Praise for Nikki Ca...

Also by Nikki Carter

Step to This
It Is What It Is

Published by Kensington Publishing Corporation

it's all good

A So For Real Novel

nikki carter

KENSINGTON PUBLISHING CORP.

www.kensingtonbooks.com

DAFINA BOOKS are published by

Kensington Publishing Corp.
119 West 40th Street
New York, NY 10018

All Kensington titles, imprints, and distributed lines are available at special quantity discounts for bulk purchases for sales promotion, premiums, fund-raising, educational, or institutional use.

Special book excerpts or customized printings can also be created to fit specific needs. For details, write or phone the office of the Kensington Special Sales Manager: Kensington Publishing Corp., 119 West 40th Street, New York, NY 10018. Attn. Special Sales Department. Phone: 1-800-221-2647.

Dafina and the Dafina logo Reg. U.S. Pat. & TM Off.

ISBN-13: 978-0-7582-3441-4
ISBN-10: 0-7582-3441-4

First Printing: November 2009
10 9 8 7 6 5 4

Printed in the United States of America

Acknowledgments

First and foremost, I thank God for opportunities, ideas, and the love of words. Thank you to my husband, Brent, for making the kids go outside so I can work ☺. Thank you to my children for eating spaghetti four days in a row while I finished writing. I appreciate y'all.

Thanks to all of the authors who write books for young adults and who have given me advice, support, and quotes. ReShonda, Victoria, Michelle, and Jacquelin: Thank you.

I've got the best agent ever! Thank you, Pattie, for tracking things down and sending positive vibes my way.

Mercedes, thanks for the hotness, the tight-lipped, blank stares and for being the coolest editor on the planet. I do not thank you for deadlines. No, ma'am, I do not.

Thanks to the realest crew of friends I could ever need! Afrika, Shawana, Tiffany T., Kym, Leslie, Myesha, and Brandi (make it hot): Thank y'all for the prayers, kind words, and feedback.

Thanks to all of the young ladies who are on this journey with me so far! And thanks to the moms, educators, youth leaders, and friends who are helping to spread the word. Pick up the book, tell a friend (but make them get their own copy).

Hope you enjoy!!!

it's all good

The answer is *no ma'am*. Actually, the answer is a big, fat *no ma'am*. There is no way I'm going to say yes to this foolishness, no matter how much my mother, Gwen, begs. No matter how much my aunt Elena gives me that puppy-dog stare.

The answer is no and that's final.

What is the question, you ask? Well, Aunt Elena has a big idea. She calls it a big idea, and it's big all right. A big, fat hot mess. But since she's the pastor's wife everyone, including my mother, is going to back her up.

She wants to start purity classes at our church and she wants me to recruit girls to participate. And not just girls from our church, but girls at school too. Why doesn't she just ask me to make a sign that says LAME and stick it on my forehead?

Of course, I'm down for being a member of the purity class. Because the flyness that is Gia Stokes is also the purest of pure. But I don't have any plans to go around the school announcing my virginity! That would be social suicide.

So I'm sitting here on my mother's favorite couch with my arms folded and a fierce frown on my face, while Gwen and Elena try their best to tag-team me.

"Gia, you are a youth leader! The younger girls look up to you," Elena says.

"She's right, Gia," Gwen agrees. "You would be good at this."

"Did anyone ask Hope to do this?" I ask.

I pose this question because Hope is the obvious choice. It would make sense since she is the pastor's daughter. Shouldn't she be required to endure the embarrassment of being part of the pastor's immediate family? She certainly gets to enjoy the perks!

"I did ask Hope, but she didn't want to do it," Elena replies.

I look to my mother for help. "So, she gets to refuse, but I can't?"

Gwen says, "You neglected to mention that you asked Hope and she said no. I thought the two of them were going to work on this together."

Elena laughs. "You can't expect Hope to do something like this. She's not really cut out for it. It would come across better from Gia. She's more studious."

So my aunt is pretty much calling me a lame. And lames are supposed to be virgins, right? If I close my eyes tightly and concentrate really, really hard will I be able to stop time and escape this madness?

"Are there going to be any boys in the classes?" Gwen asks.

Aunt Elena laughs. "Of course not. This purity class will culminate in a debutante ball. I've never heard of a boy debutante."

"Well, boys should learn about purity too," my mother argues.

"That will have to be something for the men to address."

You've got to be kidding me! So, not only are we going to have a purity class (which I'm sure will be uncomfortably embarrassing), but they're going to parade us around in poofy white dresses to prove that we graduated.

Good grief.

How about we talk about the reason my aunt came up with this ridiculous idea to begin with? This all started when my cousin Hope decided that she was going to go stark raving boy crazy. Now Aunt Elena is all twisted, thinking that her precious daughter is going to become a teen pregnancy statistic or something. Hence, purity classes.

Hope pretty much flipped her wig at the beginning of the school year when she chose my best friend, Ricky, as her first big crush. She and Valerie, my co-captain on the Hi-Steppers dance squad, both competed for Ricky's affection. It was utterly ridiculous.

And holla! He didn't pick either of them. I think he actually picked me! I say that I *think* he picked me because we haven't worked out all of the details on that. But, on the night of the Homecoming dance, he gave me a Tweety charm bracelet.

And that was totally something.

Clearly it was something, because you don't just buy your best friend jewelry. Especially when that best friend is the perfect choice for a girlfriend! But it's been two weeks since Homecoming and there have been no can-I-be-your-boyfriend follow-up activities. Not a note, not a wink, nothing! Not even one of those distressed "I hate that I like you" looks like that teen vampire from *Twilight*.

Nada. Zilch.

Gwen says, "I think that both Gia and Hope should recruit girls for the purity class. Y'all need to start with that fast-tailed Valerie."

Can you tell that Gwen no likee Ms. Valerie? My mother has had beef with Valerie since she gave me a makeover when I was in the tenth grade. She also helped me sneak out on a date and other assorted foolishness. So, yeah, Gwen has her reasons.

I want to remind Gwen of what Jesus would do in this scenario, but I also want to continue breathing, so I decide against it.

"Mom, Valerie will not want to be in the purity class. Plus, I don't know if she qualifies. Do you have to be a virgin to be in it?"

Because if the answer is yes, Valerie is sooo not on the recruit list. I mean, I don't think she qualifies as an actual skank or anything, but she's pretty close. We're talking major non-virginal activities.

"Absolutely!" says Elena. "The whole point of the class is to encourage young ladies who haven't taken that step yet."

I almost laugh out loud. Unfortunately, I think Hope and I are gonna have a hard time finding anyone in the junior class that will qualify. Maybe we'll start with the freshmen.

"Okay, Aunt Elena. I'll pass out a few flyers, but I'm not making any promises."

Elena kisses my cheek. "Thank you, sweetie!"

"But only if Hope has to help!" I add.

"Oh, all right," Aunt Elena says. "I'll tell Hope that she needs to assist you."

Gwen says, "Candy will help, too. The three of you will make a great team."

I groan loudly. Candy is my all-around irritating step-sister. I spend enough of my downtime with her as it is, seeing that she macked her way onto the Hi-Steppers squad. Now I have to take purity classes with her, too! So not the bidness.

My phone buzzes at my hip, taking my attention away from Gwen and Elena.

I read the text message from Ricky. **Hey you!**

See, this is what I'm talking about. What exactly does *hey you* even mean? Is that a greeting for a home girl, or for someone you're trying to holla at? I think Ricky is purposely being ambiguous (go find your dictionary, boo) so that he doesn't have to deal with the possibility of *us*.

Since I don't know if I want to deal with that either, I understand his pain. But I'm going to need him to snap out of it and declare what the whole mystery of the Tweety bracelet means.

The Tweety bracelet that I've been rocking every day like my *boyfriend* gave it to me!

I text Ricky back with an equally ambiguous: ☺

Take that, Ricky Ricardo.

"Who are you texting?" Gwen asks.

Mmm . . . kay. Why is Gwen all up in my bidness?
"Ricky."

Gwen narrows her eyes and shares a glance with Aunt Elena. "Good grief. You girls are going to ruin Ricky with all of this attention."

"I agree. He's not the only boy on the planet," Elena adds.

"Uh, I'm only responding to a text that my friend sent me. You two are completely out of control."

Why is it that when I'm finally getting my little shine on, everybody wants to throw powder on it? Nobody, especially Aunt Elena, had any problem with Hope's desperate chasing of Ricky! Did anyone tell her to pump her brakes when she was writing him twenty-page letters?

The answer is no.

Did anyone tell Hope to stay home when Ricky made it abundantly clear that he was not trying to be her date for the Homecoming dance?

Yeah . . . that would be another *no*.

So they can absolutely save the hateration. They can save it for some time in the hopefully not-too-distant future, when Ricky is actually my boo.

Oooh, hold up a second. I'm going to have to give myself a lame citation for using the early 2000 term *my boo*. Womp, womp on me!

Gwen sighs and says, "We are not out of control. You young ladies are out of control, which is exactly why I'm one hundred percent for this purity class. All this boy chasing and carrying on must cease."

Did I just roll my eyes extra hard? Yeah, I totally did.

"I agree, Gwen. It's time we put our feet down and stop this madness!"

Okay, seriously, Auntie Elena is moving her mouth and sound is coming out, but she's not making one bit of sense.

"I said I'd be on your recruitment squad! Can I please be dismissed? You two don't need me in the room to discuss the state of today's teenager!"

Gwen narrows her eyes and turns to Elena. "Do you see what I have to deal with?"

"Hope isn't any better," Aunt Elena replies.

A growl escapes my lips as I storm off to my bedroom. I plop down on my brand-new Tweety comforter and pull my phone out. It's buzzing again.

Hi-Steppers meeting in two hours at IHOP.

This time it's Valerie blowing up my phone. I already know what she wants to meet about. The Longfellow Spartans are going to the state football championship, and we have to do an extra-special routine.

Valerie should be glad she's still on the squad after what she pulled at the Homecoming game. She was extra heated that she didn't win the Homecoming Queen title and take over the halftime show. She had the drum major in the marching band give a speech about her and everything.

It was bananas!

Somehow, I think Valerie still isn't over the loss to quiet little Susan Chiang. She blames every single last person on the rally girls spirit squad, my cousin Hope included, for not getting that Homecoming Queen crown.

And if she's not over it . . . then the war is not over.

If I was one of the rally girls, I'd be taking cover. They're going to be walking down the hallway, and out of nowhere someone's going to yell "Man down!" just like Keyshia Cole's mama on that reality show.

And trust . . . it's going to be *all bad*.

★ **2** ★

Two hours later, my stepsister Candy and I walk into the gymnasium for the Hi-Steppers meeting, and everyone is already here. That's a first, because Valerie is always late. She likes to take her time and let everyone wait for her. It's all about her inner diva.

But not today, so she must be on some kind of mission. And from the look on her face, it's all bad.

"Ooo-OOO!" Valerie calls. "Thanks for showing up!"

Ooo-OOO is the Hi-Steppers' trademark. It sounds kind of like a bird call, unless you've got a deep voice, and then it just sounds a mess.

I reply, "Chill, we're only five minutes late."

"What a good example for the rest of the squad, *co-captain*."

I toss up one hand and roll my eyes. "Carry on, Valerie."

Valerie is still twisted that she's no longer the queen of the Hi-Steppers. At the beginning of the school year, our coach, Ms. Vaughn, made me Valerie's co-captain based on my ridiculous choreography skills.

I know what you're thinking. I *am* feeling myself just a little bit. Normally, that would not be a good look, but in this case, it is totally justified. Seriously!

Valerie continues, "Anyway, I was saying how we, as the Hi-Steppers, have to reclaim what's ours."

"And that would be what?" Kelani asks.

Candy and I look at each other and smile. Kelani must be sick of being Valerie's sidekick. Kelani and Jewel, the giggle twins, have generally been Valerie's little peons. She tells them to jump, and they're doing double dutch.

"Why don't you listen so I can finish?" Valerie asks. "We need to reclaim our title as the school's spirit ambassadors."

Jewel says, "I thought that the cheerleaders were the spirit ambassadors."

"What about the rally girls?" Candy adds.

"Really," I say, "we're the front line of the marching band. So, yeah, we're about spirit, but we're mostly about stepping!"

Everyone nods at my definition. Well, not everyone. Valerie looks like she wants to open a whole can of Latina whooping on me.

"We are *more* than the front line of the marching band. We get the team pumped for a victory! WE are the heart and soul of the Longfellow Spartans!"

Somebody has been watching too many Lifetime movies.

"Okay, okay. We're the heart and soul! But what does that have to do with our step routine for the state championship?" I ask.

Valerie smiles. "I'm glad you asked that, Gia. I've come up with a routine that will prove who has the most spirit."

Valerie points to Jewel, who gets up to press Play on the CD player. Rihanna's "Umbrella" plays from the speakers. Valerie does her little step, and er . . . uh . . . it is the opposite of slamming. Actually, it's la-a-a-ame.

After the music stops, I look around to see everyone's expressions. No one is impressed. At all. I don't even think Valerie was impressed with that mess.

"Well, you have to see it with the umbrellas," Valerie explains.

She is met with silence. Ha!

Should I save her? I suppose I will.

I say, "I'm with you on bringing the spirit, but what if we do a traditional military drill step to the music?"

Valerie scrunches her nose like she's not feeling it. "Military? Boo, we are fabulous. We do fabulous routines."

No, she didn't. Not after she just did a routine that looked like my three-year-old cousin's ballet recital.

"Valerie, we can do it in a totally fab way. Check this. The Spartans in Greece were warriors, so our Spartans, they're like soldiers."

Valerie rolls her eyes. "Yeah, I get where you're going with the military theme. Just hurry up and get there."

You cannot rush genius.

"Anyway," I continue, "we can get the Spartans pumped up with this." I grab my book bag and take out a CD and a whistle. I look over at Candy, who's waiting for my cue. She and I have been rehearsing this routine and it is fire, trust me.

I pop my CD into the CD player.

I say, "Kelani, when I point to you, press Play."

"What?" Valerie asks. "The music starts the routine."

"Not this one. It's military style."

I blow the whistle that I hung around my neck, then Candy and I start the routine. The beginning is a series of claps, kicks, and stomps. When we're done with this part, I point to Kelani and she presses Play.

The music starts, and it's two old school fight songs, handpicked by me. "We Will Rock You" and "Another One Bites the Dust." Yeah, totally hot.

The choreography is tight, too, but I must give props to Candy. Yes, she's my completely annoying stepsister who constantly brings the drama, but she is sooo gifted when it comes to making up these step routines. When Valerie graduates at the end of the year, I'm suggesting that Candy take her place as co-captain of the Hi-Steppers squad.

But keep that on the low. Valerie would be super twisted, and I can't have Candy getting a big head or anything like that.

Everyone claps when we finish . . . even Valerie.

"It's not what I had in mind," Valerie says, "but it's caliente, chica. Does everyone want to do Gia's step for the state championship game?"

"Candy helped, so it's not just my step," I add.

Candy looks really shocked. "Thanks, Gia."

Let me just say this. I'm really not this nice, especially to Candy. But she's going through a pretty horrific punishment right now. A few weeks ago, she got caught shoplifting and her dad, LeRon, and Gwen took all her clothes! All of her Dolce, all of her Juicy Couture, all of her Baby Phat—gone!

They left her with, like, five outfits that look like they came from Target. And that's all she can wear until spring break. So she's having the worst day ever, like every day.

Not only did they take away her clothes, but she can't participate in any Hi-Steppers events, except practice. She can't step at the game or ride the school bus to Columbus, Ohio, which is two hours from our 'hood in Cleveland, where we're spending the night after the championship game. She's on complete and total lockdown.

So let's just say that she deserves something good.

"Next practice," Valerie says, "we're going to start learning Gia and Candy's step. Also, Ms. Vaughn says we need to pick roommates for our hotel rooms in Columbus. We have to be four to a room. Gia, Kelani, and Jewel, you're with me."

"What if we don't want to be with you?" Kelani asks.

Jewel's eyes get really big, like she's about to leave her home girl hanging, and Jewel *never* leaves Kelani hanging.

Jewel asks, "Why wouldn't we want to room with Valerie?"

"I don't want to. She can room with the other seniors who don't feel they have to come to the Hi-Steppers meetings."

Whispers ripple through the group. It's true that the seniors don't come to the team meetings. A couple of them play field hockey, though, and one of them runs cross-country. They do come to practice, though, and that's the most important thing.

With the Hi-Steppers, if you don't come to practice, then you don't get to step. That's Ms. Vaughn's rule, and nobody ever tries to overstep that.

"Kelani, do you have a problem with me?" Valerie asks.

"Why do you think that?" Kelani responds.

Valerie gets right in Kelani's face. "Because your attitude has been stank with me since the Homecoming game. What's up with that?"

Jewel looks at the floor. Obviously *she* knows what's up. Somebody needs to tell the rest of us, so we can move on.

Kelani doesn't back down. "What's up with you going to Homecoming with my dude?"

Are you kidding me? Who knew Kelani was hollering at Chris, the drum major? He helped Valerie in her little scheme during the Homecoming game and she rewarded him with a date to the dance. Everyone thought it was funny—except Kelani, I guess.

Valerie laughs out loud. "I've had enough drama over these lame high school boys! Chica, I do not want Chris. He's served his purpose to me. Does anyone else have any real announcements?"

Candy raises her hand. "Yes, I do. My stepmom and step-auntie are starting purity classes at our church. Everyone is invited to join us."

"Purity classes? What are those?" Jewel asks.

I shake my head, because I know that now I have to answer this. Why did Candy open her big, fat mouth? That was soooo not a Hi-Steppers announcement.

"Purity classes are for girls who plan to keep their virginity until marriage. I guess they're gonna teach us about respecting ourselves and all that. I know it's a little lame, but . . ."

"Sign me up," Valerie says.

I blink three times before answering. "Umm . . . you have to be a virgin to be in the class."

"I *am* a virgin. Don't believe everything you hear."

I'm going to go with this for a moment. It will be a quick moment, because Valerie's reputation is pretty darn bad. But, for the sake of argument, let's say that Valerie *is* a virgin.

If that's the case, there are a lot of lying boys in this school, because I've heard that she's done everything under the sun. Things that I'm not even supposed to know are possible. Bad things that would result in Gwen ending my life.

But, who am I to say that the boys *aren't* lying? It wasn't too long ago when Romeo lied on me to everybody. He had his entire little crew thinking I was out there all like that. And I totally was not!

Here's the thing, though. If they are lying on Valerie, she doesn't seem to care one bit. I think she likes having a bad reputation.

So, tell me why someone who enjoys having a bad name would join our little purity class?

Methinks something is rotten in Denmark.

Oh, come on, people . . . Hamlet? Shakespeare? Required reading!

Anyway, I don't think Valerie will last very long in a class run by Gwen the punisher.

"Okay, Valerie," I reply, "you can come to the purity classes. They start on Wednesday evening at our church."

"Cool. Does anyone else have any announcements?" Valerie asks.

Jewel raises her hand. "The rally girls are having a pre-state party on Thursday night."

Valerie says, "Thanks for the reminder, Jewel. We'll all be there."

Hold up. Wait a minute. Before Homecoming, Valerie tried to institute an all Hi-Steppers ban on the rally girls' parties. Of course, I ignored the ban, because my cousin Hope is a former Hi-Stepper, current rally girl. Plus, they have slamming parties.

"I thought we were reclaiming our title as spirit ambassadors," Kelani says. "Can you make up your mind about what we're doing?"

Valerie gives Kelani some pretty evil side eye. Kelani is pushing it. I've only seen Valerie act civilized in very small doses. We've already been blessed with more than thirty minutes of sweet Valerie. In about five seconds she's gonna start tripping.

"Yes, we are the spirit ambassadors, but that doesn't mean we won't support other Longfellow groups. We're all one school."

If you know Valerie, like I know Valerie (and some of you do), then you know something isn't right. She has this look on her face that reminds me of Sylvester the cat, right before he tries to jump up and snatch Tweety out of his cage.

Yes, Tweety *is* a boy.

Like I was saying, Valerie has a devious expression on her face, like she knows something the rest of us don't.

Valerie says, "Everyone is dismissed from the meeting! Holla!"

Before leaving the gym, Kelani and Jewel storm over

toward me. They don't look happy. I never thought I'd see this day, when Twiddledee and Twiddledum are not on the same page.

"Gia!" Jewel says. "Are you gonna be in our hotel room?"

"Yeah, sure."

My hip buzzes. Well, not my hip, but my phone that's on my hip. It's a text.

SAT prep class starts week after next. want me to sign you up? Kev.

I reply. **Absolutely.**

"Who was that?" Candy asks.

"Nobody. Just Kevin."

"What did he want?"

"He wanted me to tell you to mind your own business."

Sometimes it's cool having a younger sister, although I'm still getting used to it. But other times, I just want to tell her to step. You know what I mean?

Kevin and I are planning to get as close to perfect scores on our SAT exams as possible. We're both trying to get full scholarships to college, because we're not exactly from privileged families. Ricky will probably get an athletic scholarship, although he really wants to go to Morehouse to study medicine.

I haven't decided where I want to go yet. I might go the Ivy League route and take all this fabulousness up to Brown or Columbia. Or, I might do the whole historically-black-college thing. If I go to Spelman, Ricky and I can kick it like on that old-school television show *A Different World*. That would be the hotness.

Candy and I walk out of the gym and Ricky is waiting outside for us. He's posted up on his rusty Pontiac like he's been waiting all day.

I stop in front of him and say, "I didn't know you were picking us up."

"I'm picking *you* up," he says with a smile. "Candy's going with Valerie."

"Wha . . . ?"

I turn around to see Candy jogging toward Valerie's car. I know she thinks she's doing me a favor and getting out of the way. Normally I would appreciate it, but with the way Ricky's been acting, I don't know.

"Come on, Gi. We're meeting Kevin up at the mall. He wants us to go shopping with him."

"Shopping? For what?"

"Gear. He got his birthday money from his grandparents, and he's trying to maintain his new look. He liked the attention he got at Homecoming."

Well, of course Kevin got attention at Homecoming. I totally dressed him. Kevin, Ricky, and I had a little color scheme going, because we had a dance step. Kevin didn't actually dance, but he hyped everyone up. It was bananas.

Ricky opens the car door for me. "Get in."

I stand here for a moment, trying to figure out if I appreciate this bossiness from Ricky.

"Are you coming with me?" Ricky asks.

"If you ask nicely."

A smile creeps up on Ricky's lips. "Will you please get in the car, Gia? Kevin is waiting on us."

"Sure."

I climb into the car and allow Ricky to close the door. I have an inner chuckle when I see the little cherry air freshener hanging from Ricky's rearview mirror. That's the only thing in this car that's new. Everything else is about twenty years old. I'm actually surprised that this hoopty even runs.

"Gia, I need to ask you something," Ricky says as he puts the car in drive.

Is this it? Is this when he's going to cut the games and ask me to be his girl?

"Ask away."

"You're not going to start acting all weird because of that bracelet, are you?"

I swallow hard. This is so not what I was trying to hear. "What? No! Why would I act weird?"

"I don't know. The bracelet doesn't mean that we're kicking it or anything like that. I just thought you would like it."

I roll my eyes to the sky. Who knew that Ricky was a huge coward? He can lead the football team to the state championship, but can't even admit he has a crush?

"Yeah, cool, Ricky. I get it."

I blow air out of my cheeks and look out the window. I really want to throw something and spazz out, but I refuse to let Ricky see me sweat him.

"Are we cool?" Ricky asks.

"Yep, it's all good."

"Great, because I have another question."

I roll my eyes. "Go ahead."

"Are you going to get a driver's license anytime soon? You've wasted your entire sixteenth year!"

So here's the thing about the whole driver's license debacle: I am afraid to drive. The thought of pressing the gas pedal and several tons of metal and rubber speeding down the street at my command is absolutely terrifying. I'm perfectly fine bumming rides from Kevin and Ricky. I don't *need* my driver's license.

"I'll get it sometime this year, I guess."

"Do you want me to teach you to drive?"

"Um, no!"

Ricky smiles. "Gia, it's not hard! Let me just take you up to Easter Hill Park and you can get a feel for the car."

"Naw, I'm chill right now, Ricky. I'll get it before I leave for college! Don't sweat it."

Even if I did want Ricky to teach me to drive, I'm not agreeing to it right now! Not when he just burst my fragile little crush bubble. Asking me if I'm going to start acting weird!

Wow! He gets the I-hate-you-so-much-right-now side eye. How could he?

★ 3 ★

"I don't think so, Kevin. Step away from the overalls," I say as I grab the stonewashed farmer pants out of Kevin's hands.

"What's wrong with overalls?" Kevin asks. "I like them, because they're kind of like shirt and pants at the same time."

Ricky laughs. "Kev, that's exactly the problem. Listen to Gia on this one. Trust."

"How about these?"

I hold up a dark pair of Sean John jeans. Not the baggy kind, because that's so not Kevin. He was raised by old people, so he won't wear a pair of pants that don't sit on his waist. I'm surprised he doesn't wear suspenders.

Kevin takes the jeans from me and looks at them. "I guess these are okay," he says.

"You guess? Kevin, these jeans are hot to infinity. Go try them on."

Kevin smiles. "Wow, you're bossy!"

"And?"

"Nothing. Boss me anytime."

"Ewww, Kevin. Just go try on the jeans!"

Ricky and I stand near the fitting room while Kevin goes inside. I haven't said a word to Ricky since we were in the car because I cannot believe the foolishness that was the conversation we just had. I want to take this *nothing* bracelet and throw it at Ricky.

"Gia, are you mad at me?" Ricky asks.

"Why would I be mad at you?"

"I don't know, but you seem angry."

I shrug. "I don't know what you're talking about. Are you sure you aren't going to start acting weird?"

Ricky sighs and looks at the floor. "Nah."

Kevin comes out of the fitting room wearing the jeans and they look really good on him.

"Gia, would you holla at me if I was wearing these jeans?" Kevin asks.

I laugh out loud. "Um . . . the jeans don't make the man."

"So that's a no?"

"It's a no."

"Do you think Candy would holla at me?" Kevin asks, suddenly sounding quite serious.

Why would he want to talk to Candy? First of all, she's a freshman. Second of all, she's got a little shoplifting habit. Third, and most importantly, she's not me. How could Kevin go from loving me to crushing on Candy? That's a significant downgrade, on the real.

"Kevin, when did you get so girl crazy?" Ricky asks.

Kevin replies, "Dude, you are cool enough to say that

you don't have a girlfriend because you don't want one. But people think I don't have a girl because I can't get one."

Kevin is referring to Ricky's declaration that he doesn't want a girlfriend, because he doesn't want to be pressured by fast girls. Yeah, I was down with his decision and all, when he was talking about Valerie, but there would be absolutely no pressure if he dated me!

"Who cares what people think?" Ricky asks.

"Only cool people don't care what people think," Kevin replies. "The little people care."

I hand Kevin a shirt to go with his jeans. "Oooh, that's fiyah! You like?"

"Yeah, that's cool. I'm gonna wear this on the bus when we go to state."

The band is big enough that they get their own school bus when we go to the state championship. The Hi-Steppers, the band's front line and *Longfellow spirit ambassadors* (cheerleaders hahaha), get to ride on the band bus.

I say, "If you wear that, then I'll sit next to you on the bus."

Kevin's eyes light up. "Seriously? You're not kidding, are you, Gia? Because if you were, that would be mean."

"I'm not kidding."

"Cool. Are we sitting up front or in the back? I like sitting in the front, because that is the safest, but if you want the back, I'd be totally cool with that, too. You know what? I'll get there early to save us a seat."

"Kevin . . ."

"Yes, bus partner?"

"Don't make me change my mind."

★ 4 ★

"**H**e actually said that?"

Hope is perched on the side of my bed listening to me rant about Ricky's foolishness. I called her and she came over once I got back from the mall. All I want to do is take this Tweety bracelet off and throw it across the room. I mean, why shouldn't I? It doesn't mean anything.

And it totally kicks rocks that I don't have anyone but Hope to talk to about this. Just a few weeks ago, she was all up on Ricky, so any advice she might give is suspect, to say the least. But it's either Hope, Candy, or Kevin.

Candy is an absolute no, because she's a freshman. What the heck does she know about complex relationship questions? And Kevin is just a no. There is no explanation needed.

So, yeah. It's Hope.

"Yes, he actually said that," I reply. "Can you believe he asked me if I was going to start acting weird?"

"Well, you are acting kind of weird, Gia."

See what I mean! Suspect beyond belief.

"How am I acting funny?"

Hope explains, "You're all stressed about this Ricky crush. It's not like you haven't always kinda dug him, so why is it such a big deal now? Why can't y'all just be the same?"

She is so dense. How can it ever be the same? Ricky has taken a step into boyfriend territory. You can't just come back from that. It's like saying you've never tasted pizza after you've already taken a bite and have cheese hanging off the side of your mouth.

"I'm not stressed. I just need to know what's going on. You don't just buy someone jewelry and then start tripping."

Hope nods. "I do agree with you on that. Ricky shouldn't have given you that if he didn't want to send out the wrong signal."

"I don't think he sent out the *wrong* signal. I just think he's not ready to handle it yet. He sent out the right signal, but now he wants to take it back."

Hope is wading very close to the hater side of the swimming pool. She's just mad because Ricky wasn't sending her any signals at all.

Hope shrugs. "Well, whatever, Gia. You know Ricky better than I do. I don't know why you asked for my opinion anyway, because you definitely don't want it."

"You're right, I don't. Change the subject before I kick you out of my room."

"You are evil," Hope says.

"Right back at cha, ma."

There is a light knock on my bedroom door. It has to be Candy because Gwen does not knock. She doesn't believe in teenagers having privacy.

"What do you want, Candy?" I ask through the closed door.

Candy replies, "Stop being mean and let me in! I'm bored."

I roll my eyes and flop onto the bed in *my* room. When Gwen and LeRon first got married, this was LeRon's office and he was not trying to give it up. I had to share a room with Candy, and I most definitely did not appreciate that ridiculousness.

We had bunk beds and everything.

Me no likee!

Then LeRon found himself some "get right." Yeah, I don't know exactly what this means, but my mom always says it when I'm acting crazy and then pull myself together. Bottom line is, I got my own room. Woo-hoo!

And guess what? Annoying little sisters are only admitted on a case-by-case basis.

Hope jumps up from my bed and opens the door. "Come on in, Candy. Gia's acting stank anyway, so I'm not sure if you want to come in."

Candy narrows her eyes over in my direction. "What is your issue?"

"I don't have any issues. You and Hope can fall back immediately."

"She's tripping because Ricky hasn't asked her to be his boo yet," Hope responds, as if I've said nothing.

Candy nods. "Well, that's typical boy behavior."

"And how do you know?" I ask.

"I watch *The Tyra Banks Show!* Guys put themselves out there and then they get scared. Ricky had an aha moment when he gave you that bracelet, and now everything else is brand-new. He's just scared."

Hope and I stare at Candy in shock. Tyra show reference aside, she actually sounds credible. Could this be some sort of fear mechanism kicking in for Ricky? And if it is, should I let him off the hook or proceed? So many questions . . .

"For real, though, Candy. Maybe you're watching too much Tyra," I say. "An 'aha moment'? Seriously?"

Candy laughs. "Actually, the aha moment is from my other mother, Oprah."

See, this is why I keep the door to my bedroom closed.

★ **5** ★

It's Wednesday night and I'm sitting in the church social hall waiting for our very first purity class to start. Yay! (Do you detect a hint of sarcasm? HA! That would be *more* than a hint, thank you very much.)

I look around the room to see who decided to join us. Of course, Candy and Hope are here. They, like me, didn't have a choice. Valerie's here, too, looking like a pariah because nobody's sitting next to her. No, not *Mariah*. Pariah.

Also in the room is fellow junior, Sascha Cohen. She's one of Hope's rally girl friends, which means that maybe Hope decided to open up her mouth about the program. Sascha's really pretty. Her mom is this tiny Filipino lady and her dad is Black. Sascha took the best traits from both her parents, it seems. She's tall and brown like her dad, but has almond eyes and long wavy hair like her mother. She's cool, so I'm really glad she came.

There are some other girls from our church, too, probably being forced to attend by their mothers.

"Sascha, come sit over here with us!" Hope says.

Sascha smiles and joins us. Candy appraises her outfit with a bit of envy in her eyes. I don't know if she's gonna make it through her punishment. Her lack of fly apparel seems to be killing her.

"That skirt is cute," Candy remarks.

"Thanks," Sascha replies. "And thank y'all for asking me to sit over here. I thought Valerie was gonna come and sit next to me."

Hope jumps up and hugs Sascha. "I would never leave a rally girl hanging! You know this."

Gag on top of gag. I'm so sick of Hi-Steppers this and rally girls that. Are you kidding me? I really despise cliques, and yet I seem to reside amongst them. Go figure.

Aunt Elena and Gwen emerge from somewhere in the back of the church sanctuary. They must think they are too cute with their little yoga outfits on. I guess they're supposed to be on our level, so they didn't wear their usual church outfits. My mother usually wears a hat wide enough to poke somebody's eye out every time she sets foot inside the church. And Aunt Elena stays rocking some kind of Banana Republic suit.

"Hello girls!" Aunt Elena says. "We are so happy that you joined us for PGP!"

PGP? Oh, no. They done went and made up an acronym. I'm afraid to know what the letters stand for, and from the way Hope is covering her face with both hands, she's afraid, too.

Gwen exclaims, "I bet you're all wondering what PGP stands for!"

"It stands for Powerful Girls are Pure!" Aunt Elena says, and then she gives Gwen a high five.

Kill me. Kill me now.

"We are about to embark on a wonderful journey!" Gwen exclaims.

Aunt Elena nods. "Absolutely. You young ladies are about to experience the passage into womanhood."

Oh wow! Talk about laying it on thick. The Gwen and Aunt Elena tag team is in full effect. The fact that they've put their differences aside to mold the minds of young women is inspiring.

Um . . . yeah.

I'm just waiting for Aunt Elena to say something out of pocket to or about Atilla the Gwen. That's when things will get interesting.

Gwen opens a huge shopping bag and says, "First Lady Elena and I have a gift for each one of you!"

No, Auntie Elena is not the president's wife, silly! In our church, we call the pastor's wife First Lady. Now pay attention before you miss something.

Gwen reaches into her bag and pulls out a handful of plastic tiaras.

"While we're in class, each of you will wear one of these tiaras, because you are daughters of King Jesus," Aunt Elena explains.

Gwen adds, "And that makes you princesses!"

Why are Aunt Elena and Gwen clapping and giving themselves a round of applause? They are just too proud of themselves.

"During our sessions, you will address each other by your royal names," Aunt Elena says. "Princess Hope, come and receive your tiara."

When we're all looking beyond foolish with plastic, dollar-store tiaras on our heads, Gwen and Aunt Elena seem pleased. At least *someone* is happy about this ridiculousness.

Womp, womp on us.

"Over the course of our time together, we're going to talk about why your minds, hearts, and bodies are precious to God," Aunt Elena explains.

Gwen says, "You will maintain exceptional conduct and grades while in the PGP program. And at the end of March you will graduate from the program and be presented at the PGP cotillion."

Aunt Elena asks, "Are there any questions?"

Sascha raises her hand.

"Yes, Princess Sascha?" Aunt Elena says with a big smile.

Sascha asks, "Is a cotillion a dance? Like a prom? And do we get to bring a date?"

Gwen replies, "It's something like a dance, but your parents will be there and you'll be presented as the debutantes that you are. It's going to be in early spring, because that's when the flowers start to bloom, and you will be blooming into young women."

Gag on top of gag.

Sascha scrunches her nose. "Our parents are going to be there? With our dates?"

"They won't actually be dates. They'll be escorts, and only part of the ceremony."

Sascha still doesn't look convinced. "Okay. I guess I get it."

Gwen is giving Sascha the shut-your-mouth-that's-enough-questions stare down. Candy raises her hand and lets her off the hook.

"Yes, Princess Candy?"

Candy clears her throat and swallows. "How will you know if everyone has good conduct?"

Gwen narrows her eyes at Candy. Have I taught this child nothing? Unnecessary questions always activate Gwen's mess radar!

Fortunately for Candy, Aunt Elena tackles her question. "Well, you ladies are on an honor system, as far as we're concerned. We expect you to understand that this is more about a relationship with God than a dance at the end of March. That being said, if something is brought to our attention, Sister Gwen and I may be forced to take action and you could possibly be removed from the program."

Wow. It looks like Aunt Elena and my mom are definitely not playing. Just about every girl in the room looks a tad bit uncomfortable. Valerie more than anyone else—hmmm . . . I wonder why?

I still haven't figured out why she's even here, because I sure don't believe it's all about wanting to be pure.

"That was so embarrassing," Hope says to me as soon as we're dismissed.

"Tell me about it. How and when did Gwen and Aunt Elena get so out of control?"

Candy responds, "It's not that bad. I mean, at least we get to have a cotillion out of the deal."

Right. A cotillion. Yet another dance where I have to

find a date. They can call it an "escort" all they want, but for real—it's a date. It seems like my life goes from one dance to the next, all opportunities for me to look like the lame, dateless chick.

Maybe I'll just surrender and let Kevin be my boyfriend. He's dressing better, has contacts, and his driver's license. Plus his acne is like half gone. Yeah, that still leaves an awful lot of pimples, but you know what I mean.

Hope snatches me out of my daydream . . . er . . . nightmare.

"Gia, why is Valerie here, anyway?"

"Heck if I know! Big mouth Candy brought it up in Hi-Steppers practice and she invited herself."

Hope frowns. "I think she's just here to cause trouble. She left a nastygram on Susan Chiang's Facebook page the other day."

"What do you mean, nastygram?"

"She just posted a note to her wall that said, 'Bow to the real queen of Longfellow High. It's not over.'"

I burst into spontaneous laughter. *It's not over!* Are you kidding me?

"That doesn't even sound like Valerie," I say after I'm done laughing. "She's much more cerebral than that. The whole Facebook stalking seems so juvenile."

Candy says, "I saw it, too. It was right there in my updates, next to a picture of Susan wearing her Homecoming crown."

"It was there," Sascha concurs. "We all told Susan that Valerie is just jealous and that she shouldn't worry about it."

Hmm . . . I don't know if that was good advice. If that

was truly Valerie posting a note on Susan's page, she probably *should* worry. But I still can't see Valerie sitting at home on her computer thinking up halfway mean things to say online. She's the type to get right up in your face and get you told.

Valerie waves at me and Candy from across the sanctuary as she walks out the back exit. How do I know she wasn't waving at Hope and Sascha too? That's easy.

They're rally girls.

★ 6 ★

It's Friday, and I am too pumped because I'm sitting in my last-period English class with Kevin and Ricky and it's almost over! That means that in less than thirty minutes we're going to be on the school bus and headed to Columbus, Ohio, for the state high school football championship. The Spartans are playing the Finley Sabers, and it should be a beast of a matchup. (You like that little play on words, don't you? Sabers . . . beast? Okay, whatever, hater. It was a good pun.)

Ms. Beckman, our fierce English teacher, is letting us chill until the bell, because she knows that we are way too excited to hear anything she's trying to tell us about poetry structure. That's going to have to wait until next week when the Spartans are the state champs!

Do I sound extra pumped? Hahahaha.

"Are you still gonna sit next to me on the bus?" Kevin asks.

He is most definitely rocking his new outfit and a fresh haircut, so I guess I'll keep my word. "Sure, Kev. Too bad Ricky's gonna be on the other bus. He's gonna be so bored without us."

Ricky chuckles. "I'm sure I'll manage."

Can I tell you that he really, really is starting to get on my nerves? I'm trying to keep a positive outlook on this whole Gia/Ricky thing, but it seems like Ricky is dead set on there being no *us*.

"So, Ricky, when are the 'rents coming down?" I ask.

"They're driving down Saturday afternoon. My dad has to work in the morning. Is your mom coming?"

I shrug. "I would rather she didn't."

"Why not?" Ricky asks. "It's not like you've got any wildin' out planned. Or do you?"

"Anyway!" I say, totally dismissing Ricky. "Kev, did your grandmother pack any snacks for us?"

Kevin's face lights up, like he's really excited that I'm looking forward to riding next to him on the bus. Why you playing, though, Mother Witherspoon makes some slamming goodie bags. As long as she doesn't make those . . .

"Yes! She made us fried chicken sandwiches."

Fried chicken sandwiches.

Ricky cracks up. "Kev, you've been walking around all day with fried chicken in your backpack? It's probably spoiled by now. You and Gia are gonna end up with salmonella poisoning."

"For your info, Mr. Quarterback, I put them in the refrigerator in the teachers' lounge this morning. I'm going to warm them up right before we get on the bus."

Still giggling, Ricky replies, "Good, then. It sounds yummy. I'll take Mickey D's."

I am completely unwilling to join in Ricky's laughter. "Whatever, hater. Kevin, those sandwiches are probably going to be good. Thanks for thinking of me!"

"Anytime, Gia," Kevin replies. "I'm just glad my grandmother is letting me go. Do you know she asked Pastor Stokes if he thought there was going to be any tomfoolery on the trip?"

I see that blank expression on your face. Yeah, I don't know what tomfoolery means either. You'll have to ask Mother Witherspoon. Knowing her, she's praying against any and all tomfoolery and whatever else Kevin might get into.

Obviously, she doesn't know she's got a lame for a grandson. Kevin wouldn't know tom or foolery if they sat in his lap and patted him on the head!

Ricky slaps Kevin on the back. "It's cool, though, Kev. You're going now, and we're gonna have fun this weekend."

Kevin nods. "This is going to be my last weekend of fun for a while."

"Why is that?" I ask.

"Gia! Did you forget our SAT prep class? I signed you up, and I'm going to be driving you every Saturday. My grandmother already talked to your mom."

"All right! Spelman, here I come."

Ricky frowns and asks, "Why didn't y'all sign me up?"

"I didn't think you'd want to go," Kevin replies. "That's me and Gia's thing. We've been studying for the SATs since the eighth grade."

Kevin is telling the absolute truth. He and I have been learning SAT vocabulary words for the longest. We even picked our class schedules based on what would help us most on the test.

Ricky nods slowly and starts to scribble in his notebook, with the frown still in place. Is someone feeling left out? Better yet, is this jealousy I detect?

The bell rings and we rush out of the classroom, not waiting for Ms. Beckman to give us an official dismissal.

Kevin turns in the direction of the teachers' lounge and says, "I'll see you on the bus, Gia."

"Okay."

Ricky is still standing in front of me, giving me evil side eye.

"Dude, what is it?"

"G, I can't believe you didn't sign me up for the SAT prep. You know I never think to do stuff like that. I'm going to college too!"

Am I his mama or something? Dang! Why do I have to remember to do stuff for him? I'm *obviously* not his girlfriend, so someone please explain. What part of the game is this?

"Seriously, Ricky, there will be another SAT prep. Just get in the next class. Not a big deal."

"It's not a big deal that my two best friends are gonna be totally missing in action for the next eight Saturdays?"

Okay, so I didn't think about it that way. Ricky, Kevin, and I do usually hang at the rec center or the mall on Saturdays. We even let Hope come along sometimes. The SAT is breaking up our trio.

"You said you wouldn't act weird, Gia. I should've known that you'd act like Hope when I gave you that bracelet."

I don't know what's more insulting. The part where he said I was weird or the part where he said I was acting like Hope. He's tripping on both counts.

"For the last time, I'm not acting weird. It was an oversight, Ricky, not a conspiracy. For real."

Finally, he looks like he believes me. "It's cool, Gia."

I give Ricky what I believe is a much-needed hug. "I'm sorry about Saturdays, Ricky. We'll hang after the class lets out."

"Maybe I'll just hook up with Valerie on Saturdays."

Yeah. Not funny. Not even a little bit.

"Boy, you better quit acting stupid and get focused! You have a game to play tomorrow."

"All right, Gia. I'll see you at the hotel if I get on the bus before you. Enjoy your fried chicken sandwich."

"Ha ha. You are just full of funny today, aren't you?"

I dash to my locker to grab my overnight bag. Thank goodness, I said all of my good-byes to my mom and LeRon this morning. I so don't want to be the girl whose mom is waving at the bus as we pull off.

Hope and Candy are waiting for me at my locker. Candy looks extra heated, probably because she's not going to the game. I wonder if her punishment is really going to last until spring break. I mean, okay, yes, shoplifting is a horrible crime, but have the parental units ever heard of parole or time off for good behavior?

I'm just saying.

"I wish we got to ride the bus," Hope complains as I open my locker.

Technically, the rally girls are not a school-sponsored activity. They get to perform at the pep rally and sometimes get to decorate for school dances, but when it comes down to school budget money, the rally girls get nada, not even a ride to the state championship on the hoopty school bus.

"Who's driving you guys?" I ask.

"Sascha's older sister, Abigail. She's bringing Sascha's boyfriend too, and she's even getting a hotel room for us. It could've been you driving us if you'd get your license!"

I roll my eyes. "Hope, okay, you need to stop. You are old enough to be driving, too."

"But you know my dad won't let me drive anywhere. Auntie Gwen would sooo let you use her car sometimes."

Clearly Hope does not know her auntie. "Anyway, you said Sascha's boyfriend is coming. Who is she kicking it with?"

"This senior named Chase. You know him?"

I give Hope the are-you-kidding-me look. Of course I know Chase. He's one of the hottest white boys at Longfellow High. He looks just like that dude from *Pirates of the Caribbean*. No, not Captain Jack Sparrow! Johnny Depp is like old enough to be my grandfather. Ewww. Wait. Double ewww!

Chase looks like Orlando Bloom. He's got that dark brown hair, intense brown eyes, and that grungy boy swag. Yeah, hotness to infinity.

Candy interjects, "He is fine! She's so lucky."

Hope shrugs. "He's all right. Not really my type though."

"Well, I'd rather ride with Sascha's sister than share a seat with Kevin, eating greasy chicken sandwiches all the way there."

Candy says, "Both of y'all can bite my hotcakes because at least you're going to the game! I'm gonna be sitting at home in lameville."

Bite her hotcakes? Umm . . . what?

"I'm gonna need you not to come up with slang nobody uses but you," I command.

Candy looks confused for a sec. "Oh, you mean hotcakes? That's something me and Valerie came up with on Facebook. It's code for when guys are checking out the goods."

"You and Valerie are just becoming BFFs, aren't you? What's that about?"

Candy shrugs. "I don't know why everyone acts like she's so scary. Valerie is cool most of the time."

Hope laughs out loud. "I can't wait for you to see her true colors."

"People can change, y'all. Maybe she's just sick of being mean," Candy says.

"Whateva! Tell my mom I'm gonna call her when we get to Columbus."

"All right," Candy says. "Have fun for me."

Candy trudges down the hall to the big double doors that open up to the street. She stops right outside the door to talk to some of her freshman peeps. I thought she had dropped most of her friends when she got put on her prison punishments, especially since they were the ones she got caught shoplifting with. But it looks like they're still cool.

Hope asks, "So have you and Ricky worked things out? Is he still tripping, or are y'all booed up yet?"

"Yes, he's absolutely still tripping, but I think we have an understanding, sort of."

"What's he tripping on now?"

"He was hating for a minute about me and Kev's SAT class, like we left him out on purpose."

Hope cracks up. "Are you kidding me? What a stupid thing to be hating about. But wait, did you and Kevin do it on purpose? Do y'all want some alone time?"

I punch Hope in the arm, and she flinches. "I just think Ricky is a little loco right now, that's all."

"Maybe he's girl loco!" Hope's eyes light up. "Or maybe he's just crazy about you, Gia."

I put one hand in the air. "No. Let's not go there this weekend, Hope. I'm calling a moratorium on crushes until after the game."

"Don't you go using your SAT words on me, Gia! You *know* I don't know what that means."

Ha! Of course I know. That is what makes it so much fun.

"It just means no Gia-slash-Ricky or Ricky-slash-Gia. This is all about football and the hotness that is my step at halftime."

Hope bites her lip and drops her head. I know she misses the Hi-Steppers, even if she is having fun being a rally girl.

"You know you should really rejoin the squad next year. It would be hot if we both stepped senior year."

"I don't know. Maybe. See you in Columbus!"

I watch Hope jog over to Sascha and the rest of the rally girls. I was one hundred percent serious about wanting Hope back on the Hi-Steppers squad. It's just not the same without her.

And you betta not tell her I said that!

★ 7 ★

A gigantic smile takes up half of Jewel's face as she opens our hotel room door.

"This is hot to death!" she says. "Just the three of us in this big room!"

The hotel made a mistake and overbooked their rooms, so they had to give some of the kids from Longfellow High suites instead of the normal double room. Sweet!

We lucked up because we were at the back of the line. I could almost hug Kevin for losing one of his contact lenses on the bus (I said almost). Jewel, Kelani, and I stayed behind to help him find it and guess what? It was stuck on his shirt!

Normally that would've been a big, fat BOO to Kevin, but because his nerd steez got us an upgraded room, he gets a pass.

Kelani says, "I bet Valerie would be heated if she saw our room."

"I know, right," I reply.

Jewel squeals from the bathroom. "We have a Jacuzzi tub!"

"This is just like an episode of the *Real World*," Kelani gushes. "I'm 'bout to tell my boo to come see this."

I clear my throat. "Kelani, you know what's up. We can't have any boys in our room. Not even for a minute."

"Don't be a goody-goody, Gia. You act like I'm asking Chris to spend the night or something."

Jewel pops her head out of the bathroom. "If you did, he wouldn't have anywhere to sleep!"

"Sorry, y'all," Kelani says. "I just don't want Valerie inviting him to her room. I can't stand her."

Jewel comes out of the bathroom and sighs. "I just want everyone to make up and be friends again. I don't like all this tension."

Kelani ignores Jewel, pulls out her Sidekick, and starts clicking away. I wish Gwen would give me the money to buy a phone like that. My phone looks like it should have a picture of Dora the Explorer on the back. The buttons are all big and foolish! I don't let anybody see it.

Jewel asks, "Who are you texting, Key?"

"Nobody. I'm on Facebook," Kelani replies.

"Can you just put that thing away for the weekend?" Jewel asks. "She gets on my nerves, Gia. Posting updates and surveys all the time! Ugh!"

I let out a laugh. "I'm not getting into any BFF brawls. Speaking of which, I'm supposed to be meeting my peeps in the lobby. Y'all wanna come with?"

"Sure," Kelani replies. "Let me just finish this real quick."

"What are you posting?" I ask.

"A comment about my survey, Sixteen Random Things About Kelani."

"Why sixteen?" I ask.

"Why sixteen what?"

I roll my eyes. "Why sixteen things about you? Why not twenty?"

"Because twenty is too many things and I don't like people all up in my bidness like that."

Ha! As if she had any bidness that people would want to know about.

"Girl, come on!" I know I sound bossy, but we're meeting for food, and a girl's gotta eat.

Hope, Kevin, Sascha, and Chase are chilling on the lobby couches when we get there. Only Ricky is missing from the crew. Valerie's not here either, but then she's not really a member of our clique. I guess Sascha and Chase aren't either, but since Sascha's sister drove, I guess it's cool if they hang. Sometimes she hangs and sometimes she doesn't.

"What it do?" I ask the group.

Hope sighs. "I thought you were cured of your 'hood tendencies."

"I guess not," I say with a shrug. "Kevin, where's Ricky?"

"He said he didn't wanna hang with us because he needs his rest for the game."

"What's your room number?" I ask. "I'm gonna call and see if he wants us to bring him something."

Jewel chuckles. "That's sweet, Gia. Take care of your boo!"

Grrr! See, this is why Ricky and I have been having all this BFF distress. Everyone is trying to force something to happen that Ricky clearly doesn't want. Notice that I didn't say I didn't want it! But I'm not going to force it, either.

"Whateva! Kevin, what's the number?"

"It's 507, Gia."

I do my angry sashay over to the hotel phone and dial the number.

"Hello?"

"Hey, Ricky. It's me."

"Hey, Gia. What it do?"

See! Someone embraces the coolness that is moi!

"I was . . . I mean we were just wondering if you wanted us to bring some pizza back from the restaurant?"

"Yeah, that would be cool. You know what kind I like, right?"

I smile. "Of course. Pepperoni, extra cheese, and mushrooms."

"Yeah."

"Okay, see you in a little bit—bye!"

"Wait. Gia?"

"Yes?"

"Thank you for thinking of me."

"Of course I would think of you, dude! You're my best friend."

Ricky lets out a little chuckle. "Well, I haven't been much of a best friend lately. I know I been tripping."

"It's cool, Ricky. Must be those boy hormones or something. Get some rest."

"All right, see you soon."

Now what was that all about? Was that an apology for

his foolishness of late? It sounded like it, right? Well, I'll just take what I can get.

The Pizza Palace is conveniently connected to the hotel, so we don't have to go far. There are Longfellow Spartans everywhere. We're seriously taking over up in this piece.

Our entire group crowds into a super-large booth. Chase is sitting so close to Sascha that she might as well be in his lap, and she looks uncomfortable. Did she forget to tell her dude that she's in a purity class?

Jewel asks, "So, Hope, what do the rally girls have planned for the game? I know y'all are doing something special."

"We just made a bunch of signs," Hope replies. "We're going to do a lot of chanting and a lot of stomping! That's it."

"Y'all decided to fall back, and let the Hi-Steppers do our thing, huh?" Kelani asks. "It's about time."

Hope laughs. "Yeah, I wanted to let my cousin get her shine on."

"Whatever, Hope!" I object. "I'm always in shine mode, no matter what your status. Recognize!"

Hope sticks her tongue out at me. "Whatever, yourself!"

My miniature tiff with Hope is interrupted by Sascha. "Stop, Chase!"

Okay, I don't know what she's fussing about, but Sascha looks heated for real. Chase has this *what did I do?* expression on his face. I wonder what that's about, and I think everyone else does too, because we all totally stop talking.

"All right, chill, girl," Chase says. "I'm just playing."

"Well, it's not funny," Sascha replies.

"What's not funny?" I ask the question that everyone else probably wants to ask.

Sascha replies, "N-nothing. I'm about to go to the bathroom. Chase, can you let me out?"

Chase rolls his eyes and flings his half-greasy bang out of his face. He stands up and lets Sascha out, but he takes his time doing it. Dude has a serious attitude.

"I'm going with you," I say.

Chase narrows his eyes in Sascha's direction. Her nonverbal reply is a nod. I don't know what just went on between these two, but I for dang sure am about to find out. Number one, Sascha is my girl and I'm trying to look out for her. And number two, I'm nosy like that.

When we're in the bathroom, Sascha doesn't go into a stall. She just runs water in the sink and washes her face with a wet paper towel.

"What's up, Sascha? Everything okay with you and Chase?"

Sascha smiles, but it's not a happy smile. "Yeah, it's cool, Gia. We've been going together since freshman year, and he's starting to trip about some stuff."

"What kind of stuff?" I ask.

"Well, he's been pressuring me, because he wants me to be his first. He can barely keep his hands off me sometimes, but I don't want to hook up."

"I totally understand. Did you tell him about the purity class?"

She shakes her head. "I tried to, but he doesn't listen to me half the time anymore. I keep thinking we should break up, but I really love him, Gia."

"You do? How do you know?" I ask.

I really want to know the answer to this question. I hear people saying they're in love all the time, and I don't know what that's supposed to mean. My mom says that teenagers don't know what being in love means, but she's not right about everything.

Sascha hugs herself. "It's so intense. It's like I wouldn't want to live if he wasn't my boyfriend, Gia!"

Hmmm . . . I don't know what I think about this. I know I've never felt this way about anyone. Definitely not Romeo and not even Ricky.

"Well, what if he breaks up with you because you won't give him your virginity?"

Sascha grabs both my arms. "I don't know, Gia! I don't even want to think about it. It would be awful."

Tears come to her eyes, as if the thought of a breakup is too much for her to handle.

"Do you want to talk to my mom about it?" I ask. "She usually has good advice."

"No. Chase would be mad if I told anyone. He'd be mad if he knew I was telling you. Please don't tell anyone!"

"Um . . . okay, I guess."

I don't like making promises to keep secrets. Especially if I think Gwen would go off on me if she found out I was keeping one.

"Thank you, Gia. You'll understand when you start dating someone for real. Like Ricky, maybe? Everyone thinks y'all already go together."

"Well, we don't. We're just friends, so everyone can fall back."

Sascha laughs. "Okay, sorry!"

The pizza is on the table when Sascha and I come back and it's already half devoured. It didn't seem like we were gone that long, but apparently it was long enough for my peeps to inhale half the pizza. I'm gonna have to order Ricky's slice separately.

Besides grubbing, it looks like something really funny went down, because everyone is in some stage of laughter. Hope is clutching her stomach and Jewel has tears streaming down her face. The only one not laughing is Kelani, and, as usual, she's on that Sidekick.

"What is so funny?" I ask as I sit down.

Out of the corner of my eye I watch Chase stare Sascha down *hard*. She doesn't even make eye contact with him and she looks totally scared. Me no likee. And me definitely no likee how he snatches her arm and pulls her into the booth. No one else seems to notice this but me. They're too busy laughing.

"Is someone going to tell me and Sascha the joke?" I ask.

Hope pulls herself together and says, "We're playing Would You Rather, and the question was, would you rather have a freakishly big smile or a freakishly little nose? And Kevin . . ."

Hope bursts into a flurry of laughter.

Kevin rolls his eyes. "I just said I'd want the freakishly big smile because then I'd just look extra friendly. And then Hope tried to imagine me with a freakishly big smile and started laughing! Not even funny."

A picture pops into my head of Kevin with a huge smile and holding a greasy bag with chicken sandwiches in it. Next thing I know, I'm laughing too.

"All of you get on my nerves!" Kevin mumbles. He crosses his arms and pouts. What a diva!

By the way, I'd take a freakishly big smile if I had to choose. I'd just mean mug everybody all the time and never, ever smile!

★ **8** ★

A shiver runs through my body as I sit in the bleachers with the rest of the Hi-Steppers. It's times like these when I wish this skirt had a little bit more material, and that these shiny dancer tights were long underwear. I brush away a big, fat snowflake as it plops into my lap.

Ugh! It's cold.

Ricky's parents are here finally, and also huddled in the cold. When they didn't make it in the early afternoon like they planned, Ricky was in panic mode. He called them about fifty times asking if they'd left.

I think all of the Longfellow Spartans are happy that they showed up because my boy was tripping for real.

Valerie plops down next to me and shakes a pile of snowflakes out of her hair. "This weather sucks," she says.

"Tell me about it. But it is November, so what do you expect?"

"True. Did you see the rally girls and those lame signs?

They so are not the spirit ambassadors. I don't know how anyone got confused."

"This whole hate-the-rally-girls thing you've got going has to stop. I heard you're even terrorizing rally girls on Facebook. What's up with that?"

Valerie tilts her head to one side. "Who said I was terrorizing rally girls on Facebook?"

"Nobody important," I reply, not willing to give out any sources.

"I thought you knew me better than that, Gia. I guess not."

I roll my eyes. "I don't think anyone cares about this whole spirit ambassador mess but you, Valerie. You and maybe Hope."

"Of course I care. This is my last time wearing the Hi-Stepper boots. Not like anyone *cares* about that either!"

I put one hand over my mouth! I totally forgot that this is Valerie's last game. Unless we do a parade or something in the spring, this is it for Valerie's Hi-Steppers reign of terror.

I wrap my arms around Valerie and give a little squeeze. "Aw, Valerie. I'm gonna miss you next year."

"Yeah, right. You're gonna be so happy that I'm gone."

"I'll only be happy about being the captain all by myself. Senior year is gonna rock."

"Well, I won't be missing y'all. I'm gonna be too busy scoping out the college guys and trying to pledge a sorority."

"I didn't hear anything in the mix about learning and education."

Valerie laughs. "Girl, please. I'm going to college to find

my husband. It'll either be an athlete or a nerd. Both make the long dough. You know what I mean?"

"No, and I don't think I want to know."

Are we actually having a real friend-like conversation with no ulterior motives attached? Have Valerie and I moved to a new level in our friendship?

Valerie asks, "So, do you know what's up with Kelani? Is she really mad at me about Chris?"

I should've known there was something.

"I don't know what's up with Kelani. But I do think she thinks you're after her boyfriend."

Valerie shakes her head and sighs. "Okay, so here's the thing. I *did* let him kiss me, and then he got all sprung and started acting stupid. He actually broke up with Kelani until I said I didn't want him. Then her little desperate self took him back."

"What? Are you serious? Where in the heck have I been? I didn't know all this was happening."

Valerie chuckles. "You were in Rickyland, drooling over your little almost-boyfriend."

Almost-boyfriend!!!! Grrr . . .

"I was absolutely not drooling over him. I'm too fly to be drooling over anybody."

Valerie high-fives me. "I know that's right, chica. Do you think I have time to go holler at some of those cute Finley boys? A couple of them are looking real nice."

I shake my head. "You better hurry up! If the game starts and you're not back, Ms. Vaughn might go ballistic."

"True, true, and true. I think I do have time, though."

Valerie hops up from the bleacher and pops her booty through the crowd, making the signature Hi-Stepper call, ooo-OOO! She sounds pretty lame doing it alone, but for some reason, I don't think the boys care.

The football team comes out onto the field with Ricky leading the way. The crowd goes wild as the future state champions wave at the crowd. I watch Ricky scan the stands for his parents and a huge smile bursts onto his face when he sees them. I wait for him to look my way, too. We make eye contact and he holds one fist in the air. I pump my fist in reply. We're like a teenage Barack and Michelle Obama! Can you see me rocking a fly afro in the White House? That would be hawt!

Would I be a bad BFF and almost-girlfriend if I tell you that I am not paying attention to this football game? I mean, they're running up and down the field and scoring points, but I'm thinking ahead to halftime. I always get a little nervous right before we do a new routine.

When the halftime buzzer rings, the Longfellow Spartans are barely ahead, 14 to 12. But we've got more momentum because we scored two touchdowns, and the only points the Finley Sabers put on the board were field goals.

The Finley marching band does their halftime show first, and it is not the bidness. First of all, the band has about thirty members, and the drill team looks like a bunch of hoochies. I'm serious. I would describe their routine as exotic dancer meets Beyoncé.

Like I said, not the bidness.

When it's our turn, we storm the field like an army. Our band is huge, and that's not counting the twenty-two Hi-Steppers. We're fierce, for real.

As usual, our routine is flawless. Or, I should say, mostly

flawless. Kelani missed a crossover and a few of her claps were late. Maybe if she paid attention to the music instead of mean mugging Valerie the whole time, she would've done better.

Valerie is tripping, too. She's got her normal Hi-Stepper's smile on, and girlfriend went overboard with the Vaseline on her teeth. But she's got tears streaming down her face. Awww . . . she really is sad that her Hi-Steppers era is over. Who knew she could be so emotional?

As we march off the field, I tap her on the shoulder and ask, "You cool?"

She nods, but stays silent.

Someone from the stands shouts, "Ooo-OOO!"

Valerie grins, pumps her fist and hollers back, "Ooo-OOO!"

The rest of the Hi-Steppers follow Valerie's lead and yell back at the stands. The tears still run down Valerie's face, but she's smiling extra hard.

Since she can't leave her fans without a little *extra*, Valerie pops her behind the rest of the way off the field. Boys from both schools show their appreciation by cheering and whistling.

What part of Powerful Girls are Pure is this? Gwen would not be pleased. I'm just saying.

Now that we've got the halftime routine out of the way, I can be a real BFF and pay some attention to my boy Ricky and the rest of the team.

The second half of the game starts off with a bang and an early turnover by the Finley Sabers. The Spartans return it for a touchdown because they got it like that.

On the next Spartans possession, Ricky leads the team up the field, but the drive only gives them a field goal. Are you impressed by my football knowledge? Yeah, me too. Ha!

The Sabers aren't going down without a fight, though. They get a touchdown the very next time they get the ball. The Spartan defense better pull themselves together real quick. Coach Rogers must be reading my mind because he takes a timeout.

While the team is on the sidelines we start a "Spartans fight" chant. And the Sabers fans counter us by yelling, "Sabers roar! Grr!!!"

Grrr? Are you kidding me? We should win the game just based on the lameness of the Sabers fans. Boo!

The rally girls have pulled out flags and streamers and are lighting up the stands with red, white, and gold—the Spartans' colors.

When the team takes the field again, Ricky turns and looks into the stands. Since he's looking over in our direction, I yell, "Go Ricky!"

A huge smile bursts across his face and before I can catch myself the thought crosses my mind that he looks totally hot. Wow. My best friend is a hot boy, and apparently I'm not the only one who appreciates all his fineness. A lot of the girls cheer when Ricky smiles up at *me*.

My heart sinks a little as I have a second revelation (Ricky being a hot boy was the first). Ricky can have any of these girls. Why should he settle for me when he can have anyone else?

What if Ricky's reluctance to date has nothing to do

with purity and everything to do with playing the field? That would be all bad.

"What are you thinking about?" Kevin asks, snapping me out of my worst-case-scenario daydream.

"Nothing. Y'all did good at halftime."

"Thanks. This is fun. I hope we make it to state again next year."

"Let's get through this game first," I reply.

As if the team hears me, Ricky throws a touchdown pass to Romeo. Every Longfellow Spartans fan jumps up because it's pretty much a wrap! The Sabers are trailing by eleven points with less than two minutes in the game. As long as the Spartans defense handles their business . . .

Oh snap! Somebody missed a block because the Sabers just did a forty-one-yard run up the field. Me no likee. And neither does Coach Rogers, 'cause he's blowing whistles and carrying on like he's lost his mind.

Even from the stands we can tell that Coach Rogers is letting the defense have it, but he soooo has a good reason! We're like two minutes away from being the state champions! This is not the time to start falling apart.

The defense runs back onto the field with the Spartans fans screaming in the stands. I think we all want this as badly as the team does.

On the next snap the Spartans do what they're supposed to do! They've got the Sabers quarterback scrambling for a receiver and he can't find one.

I guess he thinks he sees an opening or maybe he's desperate, because he throws the ball directly into the hands of a Spartans defender, who runs a few yards up the field, but doesn't come close to scoring.

We run a couple of plays to take up the rest of the time on the clock, but the Spartans have victory on lock! That's what I'm talking 'bout!

When the time runs out, the entire team rushes onto the field to celebrate their victory. My heart sinks as I watch a cheerleader throw her arms around Ricky's neck and kiss him on the mouth!

Ugh! I can't believe she's putting her random germs all over him! And let's talk about how even though he *finally* pushes her away, it is totally not fast enough. I see right now . . . somebody's about to get hurt.

Let's just hope it's not me.

★ 9 ★

"**L**ook at your boy!" Hope exclaims.

I know she's talking about Ricky so I don't even want to look. He's spent this entire week being the celebrity of Longfellow High. In my opinion, he's enjoying it too much, but basketball season is here and Ricky doesn't hoop. Soon he'll be old news and maybe we can get back to normal.

"I'm not looking at him," I reply. "He's on some other stuff right now. It is so not a good look for him."

Hope laughs. "The cheerleaders think it's a good look."

Okay, why does it feel like Hope is having way too much fun with this? I know that she's still a little (or a lot) irritated that Ricky wasn't feeling her. I'm glad to see Candy walking up, because the subject needs changing quick!

"Hey, Candy. Cute outfit," Hope says.

Candy's smile beams in Hope's direction. "Thank you!"

The state of Candy's freshman fashion has been severely shattered by our parents' punishment. Any and all compliments on her limited apparel are greatly appreciated by Ms. Candy.

"Do you think Mama Gwen would be mad if I skipped the purity class tonight?" Candy asks.

"Do bears sleep in the woods?"

Hope sucks her teeth. "Gia, why can't you ever just answer a question?"

"Don't hate me because I'm witty," I reply. "Candy, why are you trying to ditch the meeting tonight?"

"Spartans Singers auditions are after school, and I don't know how long I'll be." Candy twirls the end of her long, thick braid. The twirling is a sure sign that she's up to something. This girl *stays* messy!

"Spill it," I say.

"Spill what?" Candy asks.

"The reason you're trying out for the Singers."

"I like to sing."

I twist my lips to one side. "And what else?"

"Oh, Gia, you get on my nerves!" Hope fusses. "Why does it have to be something else?"

I ignore Hope and lock eyes with Candy. "Spill it."

"All right! Chase asked me to try out."

Hope's eyebrows rise in surprise. "Sascha's boyfriend, Chase?"

"Yes. Sascha's Chase. That's why I didn't want to tell y'all. I knew you would jump to conclusions."

"We're not jumping to anything," I reply. "But when did you and Chase get to be cool?"

"One of his boys was trying to get with Valerie about a month ago. We all went out for pizza a couple of times."

Wow! Candy is sneaky as all get out. She's not supposed to have any social outings without me, but she's been kicking it with seniors behind my back.

"It sounds kind of shady," Hope says.

Candy replies, "Well, it's not, and I really hope that you two don't go running to Sascha, getting her all twisted about this."

"I'm not saying anything, but you better watch your back," I say. "Sascha says she's in love with him, so trust that she will bring the drama."

Candy rolls her eyes. "Whatever."

Candy sashays down the hallway, so I guess she's off to the audition. I'm about to continue my semi-rant to Hope, but she's clicking away on her new Sidekick. Can Gia get any technology? Yes, I did refer to myself in the third person right then, but I was having an out-of-body experience.

"Who are you texting?" I ask. "James?"

Hope and Longfellow Spartan, James, hit it off while we were in Columbus for the championship. They've been texting each other back and forth ever since. James is a cool dude. He's always full of jokes, and has a big linebacker cute kinda thing going on. He wouldn't be *my* first selection, but we are not talking about me. We're talking about Hope.

Hope's mouth hangs open, and her eyes widen as she looks at her screen. "Oh, my goodness! I do not believe this!"

"What is it?" I ask, not appreciating the suspense one bit.

"I can't believe Valerie would be this mean!"

"What!" I demand.

"Valerie posted some pictures of Susan Chiang on Facebook, and they are foul!"

I snatch Hope's phone. "What kind of pictures?"

Now my mouth is hanging open, too. The pictures look like they were taken in the shower. Most of Susan's goodies are covered, but her face looks crazy seductive, 'cause she's got her lips all pouted. When did Susan get to be one of *those* girls? She's smart, nice, and everybody likes her.

Hope says, "Valerie is pure evil. All this because she didn't get to be the Homecoming Queen?"

I rack my brain, trying to think of another reason why Valerie might hate Susan. I'm coming up with nothing but blanks. Outside of her little shower-scene photo shoot, Susan is one of the nicest people I know.

"But how do you think she got the pictures?" I ask. "Do you think she took them? She and Susan are nowhere near cool enough for that."

Hope frowns. "That's a good point. Maybe she stole them."

"Come on, Hope, Valerie is not a thief. It's not her style."

Jewel and Kelani come running down the hall. "Have y'all seen?" Jewel asks.

"Susan's pictures?" I ask.

"Yes! I hear they're talking about taking her Homecoming queen crown away," Kelani says.

Hope gasps. "No way!"

"I totally heard Ms. Vaughn talking about it in the teachers' lounge," Kelani replies.

I'm gonna need someone to explain to me how our teachers know what's posted on Facebook.

"Ms. Vaughn's got a Facebook profile?" I ask.

Kelani shrugs. "I don't know. But there are teachers on there perping as students. They are usually trying to get the scoop on cheaters and stuff."

Hmmm . . . This sounds suspicious to me, and no matter what anyone says, it doesn't sound like Valerie. Valerie is mean, but she would never do something that could be traced so easily back to herself. She's all about making people miserable without getting in trouble.

"Has anyone seen or talked to Valerie?" I ask. "Because it seems like everyone is just jumping to the conclusion that she did this."

Kelani's thick eyebrows crumple into a frown. "I didn't know you and Valerie were tight like that, Gia. You're defending her?"

I shake my head. "No. Not defending her, but I don't think we should accuse her without proof."

Jewel snatches Hope's phone and shoves it beneath my nose. "The proof's right here! It's on her Facebook profile and it says she posted it. Case closed!"

Hope takes her phone back, shuts it off and puts it in her purse. "As much as Valerie and I are mortal foes, I kind of agree with Gia. The last thing Valerie is trying to do is get in trouble and miss out on being prom queen. It's her last shot at a high school tiara."

Kelani looks super frustrated. A little too frustrated if you ask me. I mean, why is she trying to convince us that

Valerie is the devil? We already know she's got issues, but dang.

"Hope and I have a meeting at our church, so we gotta go," I say.

Jewel asks, "Oh, is that the virgin meeting?"

She and Kelani burst into a flurry of giggles. I reply, "It's our PGP group at church. Stop being haters."

"What in the world does PGP stand for?" Kelani asks.

In a voice barely louder than a whisper, Hope answers, "Powerful Girls are Pure."

"What?" Jewel asks. "I didn't hear you!"

"Oh, good grief! It stands for Powerful Girls are Pure. Now step so we can get there on time."

Kelani purses her lips and puts one hand on her hip— confrontation style. "Step? Girl, you better quit playing. You aren't dismissing anybody. You're taking that co-captain mess straight to the head."

I exhale slowly. Why must these dimmers always try to steal my shine?

"Our session today is about the one thing none of you want to talk about," Aunt Elena says.

We're in our PGP meeting and my mom and Aunt Elena have started yet another fun lesson. I happen to know that today's talk is going to be about the dangers of dating, because I saw Gwen's notes. My plan is to stay silent, not make any eye contact with my mother and get through these two hours without having to make any comments.

Yep, it's my plan and I'm sticking to it.

My mother says, "Today we're talking about dating."

Everyone groans, because nobody wants to talk about

this. Most of these girls want to talk about the dress they're wearing to the cotillion, or maybe even their escort for the cotillion. Dating rules . . . not so much.

Aunt Elena holds her side from laughing so hard. Why is the lack of enthusiasm funny?

She says, "Girls, I promise this is going to be fun. I have a question for you. What is your idea of a date?"

Valerie's hand immediately shoots up and Aunt Elena points to her. "I think a date involves food—paid for by the boy, a movie—also paid for by the boy, and maybe if it's past date number three, a kiss."

Gwen raises an eyebrow, so Valerie continues. "A very chaste, good-girl kiss, Ms. Gwen. Nothing that would get me kicked out of PGP."

"So it's not a date if the boy doesn't pay?" Aunt Elena asks.

"Not in my opinion," Valerie says.

Sascha raises her hand. "Well, I've been on a date and we each paid for our own stuff. But we were alone, so I think it was a date."

My mother asks, "So being alone makes it a date?"

"I think so," Sascha replies.

"What about you, Gia?" Gwen asks. "What do you think constitutes a date?"

Me no likee being put on the spot. My mother must've noticed my gradual slide off the church pew and onto the floor.

I clear my throat and respond. "Um . . . I think a date is whatever *you* say it is."

A slight smile teases the sides of Gwen's lips. "I'm serious, Gia."

"Well, I think a date is like a one-on-one kind of thing with a boy. But you've both got to have a crush, because that's important, too."

I had to clarify that, because I do all kinds of one-on-one stuff with Kevin, and we have not, and shall not ever be, anywhere close to having a date.

Aunt Elena replies, "I like where Gia's going with that. The whole dating ritual is about making that one-on-one connection. As adults it leads to the union of marriage."

"What do y'all think it leads to with teenagers?" my mother asks.

Someone yells out, "Baby mamas."

Gwen laughs. "That's what it led to with me! But what else? Hope?"

Hope sighs. "I guess it leads to heartbreak, because high school boys don't seem to last very long."

Aunt Elena replies, "Good answer. That's something we'll talk about later. Is there anything *good* about teen dating? I'm sure you all have begged your parents to go out on dates. What's the good part?"

"Going to the prom with an upperclassman!" Valerie blurts.

Sascha says, "Holding hands, first kisses, and finding your soul mate."

I totally give Sascha the are-you-kidding-me side eye. I think she needs a teenage love intervention. Especially when her "soul mate" is somewhat suspect.

Even Gwen is giving Sascha a blank stare. "Um, okay . . . well yes, those are all good things. We had a point to asking you all of these questions."

"We wanted to demonstrate how different people's opinions are about dating," Aunt Elena says. "Not all parents think the same and not all teenagers think alike either."

Hope raises her hand. "Well, how do you convince your parents to let you date if they don't want you to? I'm sure a lot of y'all have the same question, right?"

Everyone except Valerie answers by nodding or saying yes. She's probably the only one in our group who is actually allowed to date. The rest of us are operating in some kind of group date limbo, where we get to have a crush but only in a group setting. That kinda sucks when you're about to turn seventeen.

Sidebar. My birthday is rapidly approaching. I'll be seventeen in two weeks and not one of my friends has even mentioned the blessed occasion. I missed out on having any kind of sweet sixteen because I was totally still on punishment for sneaking out on a date with Romeo. This year, there better be some kind of celebration, or a sista like me is gonna be heated.

Now, back to your regularly scheduled drama fest.

Aunt Elena tackles the question. "I don't think it's about convincing your parents of anything. Most parents have already made up their minds about what they're going to do on the dating subject. What you can do is prove that you're trustworthy, and perhaps that will make it easier on your parents when the time comes."

Sascha raises her hand. "But what if your parents are totally unreasonable? I've been in love with Chase for years, and my mom still doesn't let me be alone on a date with him. I have to sneak, and I don't like doing that. Wait a minute, you aren't going to tell my mom I said that, right?"

My mom chuckles. "We're not going to tell anything

that's not necessary. We want you to trust us. But to answer your question, it may not seem unreasonable to your mother. Maybe the fact that you're so in love with your boyfriend makes it easier for your mom to say no."

Did anyone notice that Gwen said she wasn't going to tell anything *that's not necessary*? Umm . . . that is code for *I'm going to most definitely have a talk with your mama, you little fast-tailed heifer.* I am predicting a grounding for Ms. Sascha.

But I can totally understand my mom being like that. She would put me on total lockdown if she thought I was even close to giving up the goodies. That's why I keep her out of my bidness!

Okay, you're right. I don't really have any bidness, but that's beside the point. You know what I'm trying to say.

Aunt Elena says, "If and when you start dating, one-on-one, we've compiled a list of helpful hints. We've put them on a wallet-sized card that you can carry with you at all times."

After Aunt Elena passes out the cards, I flip the little laminated card over in my hand. It looks like they got lost in the craft store making these, but I'm not mad. Their tips are the kinds of things everybody's parents say, so I'm surprised to see most of the girls put the cards in their wallets.

Aunt Elena dismisses us with a prayer, and we all go off to our prospective gossip groups. Everyone except Sascha. She pulls my mother away from everyone and tells her something. I'm too far away to hear what she's saying, but it must be emotional, because my mom wraps her arms around Sascha and hugs her.

"What do you think that's about?" Hope asks, motioning to Sascha and my mom.

"I don't know."

And I really don't know, but I'd bet a whole bunch of somebody's money that it has something to do with Chase.

★ 10 ★

After our PGP meeting, I sit in the dining room at the computer desk and boot up. I haven't logged into my Facebook page for weeks, because with Hi-Steppers and everything else, I haven't really had any spare time.

Just to prove it, my status still says: Gia is rocking new Tweety jewelry!

I look down at the charm bracelet that I never, ever take off and think of Ricky. We haven't talked in days. I mean we chat in the hallways and sometimes eat at the same lunch table, but we haven't had a Ricky/Gia pow-wow since before the state football championship.

I leave a note on his wall. Hey Ricky. Tweety says hi!

Totally lame. I know it, but I can't think of anything that I want to say to him that will be all out in the open to his other friends. I quickly scan the notes on his wall, and of course the majority of them are from girls. Some of them are random chicks who don't even go to Longfellow High.

My cell phone rings. "Talk to me," I answer.

"Hey, Gia."

"Oh, hey, Kevin."

"Dang, you could be just a little bit excited to hear from me."

I can't even lie. I was hoping that it was Ricky. Hearing Kevin's voice on the other end was a serious disappointment.

"I'm sorry, Kev. What's up?"

"I was just confirming that I'm picking you up Saturday morning at eight forty-five."

"Kevin, the class starts at ten."

"I want to be on time," Kevin replies.

"Boo, Kevin. It's at Christ the King High School, and it's ten minutes away."

"We want a good parking spot, and a good seat in the class."

I can't even ask Kevin if he's serious, because I know he is. Kevin doesn't like being late for anything. He's never been late for school, for a class, band practice—nothing. His grandmother, Mother Witherspoon, even said he was born a day early.

"Kevin, if you ring my doorbell at eight forty-five in the morning, I'm going to be heated."

Kevin laughs. "That's good, because it's cold outside."

"Jokes?" I ask.

"Yep, and plenty more where that came from!"

As much as I don't want to, I crack up laughing at Kevin

and his silly self. It's hard to have a conversation with Kevin and *not* end up laughing. This time is no different.

"So, Gia," Kevin asks, "are you having a birthday party this year?"

"I haven't given it much thought. A party would be nice, I guess, but I'm more of a get-together kind of girl."

"So, why don't we have a get-together over at Hope's house? It would be cool if Pastor Stokes let us use his recreation room."

Umm, yeah. A birthday party at my uncle/pastor's house. Wonder how many of my school friends are gonna show up at that party bonanza? Not that I want to do anything off the chain, but I at least want people to show up.

"I don't know, Kev, maybe we could just ix nay the whole party idea."

"But . . ."

"Let's not talk about it anymore, okay?"

He must hear the finality in my tone, because he changes the subject. "Did you hear what Valerie did on Facebook?"

Okay, why does Kevin know the scoop? Whoever said that boys don't gossip is a liar. The boys I know keep up with the Longfellow drama, just like the girls. Sometimes even more than the girls, and they stay instigating.

I click over onto Valerie's page. "I saw the pictures earlier, but they've been removed."

"Yep. Susan Chiang's mother tried to get Valerie to take them down and when she didn't, she contacted Facebook and asked them to take them down."

"Well, that's good, but I don't think Valerie did it."

Kevin laughs. "Why not? She's most definitely capable of evil."

"I know, but I saw her in the PGP meeting tonight and she wasn't gloating one bit. Valerie always gloats over her victories against the lames."

"Okay, Gia, I'll give you that. But if Valerie didn't do it, then who did?"

"Good question, Kev!"

A notification pops up on my Facebook page. I click over to my wall and see this message from Ricky: Tell Tweety I miss hanging out with him.

I swallow hard and ponder my next move. Is there something between the lines here? Is this a secret declaration of love? Or is he just talking about me, him, Kev, and Hope chilling at the rec center eating microwave popcorn and drinking cocoa.

I decide not to post another note on his wall, because I'm not sure what's up. I try to *always* know what's going on in my circle. This not-having-a-clue mess is for the birds.

Kevin asks, "Okay then, Gia, I've got pre-calc homework to finish. Did you do yours?"

"Sure did."

"Well, you don't have to be so snooty about it."

The giggle escapes before I have a chance to stop it. "What? Are you mad that I'm a better student than you, Kevy-kev?"

"I don't like you right now, Gia. Talk to you later."

I press End on my cell phone. I'm about to log off the computer and find a good book to read when another notification pops up on my Facebook page. I click over to my wall and Ricky has left me another note. Somebody's about to be 17. Are we celebrating?

This I can respond to. I type: Are you throwing your BFF a par-tay?

I sit at the computer awaiting his response. Finally it pops up. Sure. I'll ask my parents.

Okay, this could end up being totally fresh. A birthday party for moi, thrown by Longfellow High's number-one hot boy.

I decide to tease Ricky a little bit. Why? Because it's what I do—especially since he's been acting crazy lately. He deserves it.

I type: Do I need to bring a date?

I can see him now, sitting at his computer with his eyebrows pulled in, looking like a caveman! He's so expressive when he's mad.

This is what Ricky writes on my wall next:

:-|

I clutch my stomach and laugh out loud. Ricky gave me the tight-lipped smiley!

Since he's determined to steer our relationship away from girlfriend/boyfriend waters and back to the shallow end of the BFF pool, then I'm allowed to tease him incessantly. (Look it up! Ha!)

Tired of tormenting Ricky, I log off Facebook and turn off the computer.

"How was PGP?" Candy asks.

Why did I not know she was behind me, reading over my shoulder? Nosy heifer. "Don't sneak up on me."

"You doing something you shouldn't be doing?" she asks.

"No. It's the principle of the matter. If we're going to be sisters, then sneaking is not allowed."

Candy laughs. "But snitching is?"

Candy went straight to the throwback of me snitching on her about her sticky fingers issue. Let's hope it's her *former* sticky fingers issue. I sure hope she's cured of that mess. She can't roll with me and my crew if she's gonna be stealing. We don't roll like that.

"Sometimes snitching is for the greater good. Not the same as sneaking."

"Whatev, Gia. Come in my room. I have something to tell you."

We have to go behind closed doors for her to tell me her news? Hmmm . . . sounds like some drama is afoot.

Once we're safely behind a locked door, she asks, "How was the meeting? What did I miss?"

"You missed out on Gwen and Aunt Elena's dating rules."

Candy's eyes light up. "Does that mean we get to go out on dates?"

"They made sure to say that the decision to allow dating is up to each parent. So, naw, they haven't said anything about allowing us to date."

"Bummer. Because I just got asked out."

"Dish! Who is it? Is it that freshman football player you've been drooling over?"

"Julian Rogers? Um, no. He's stuck up, just because his father is the coach. I can't stand him anymore."

Okay, let me translate. She tried to throw some holla in Julian's direction and got rejected. That equals him being stuck up.

"Then who asked you out?" I ask.

"Chase."

My mouth drops open. "Chase and Sascha are to-gether. I mean like, really together. Like one step away from getting married the day after graduation."

"That's not what he said. He said that Sascha is start-ing to be a drag, and he's going to tell her he wants to start seeing other people."

"A drag how?"

"She's super clingy and always talking about being in love and all that noise. Chase isn't on that right now."

I bite my lip and put my thinking face on. "Chase doesn't seem like your type. He's kind of grungy."

"Girl, he is hot to death. And he and his boys are start-ing a band in Chase's garage. He might want me to sing with them."

Who is this girl?

"Does Valerie approve of him?"

Candy laughs. "Who cares what Valerie thinks? She's about to graduate in June. I was just cool with her while we were on Hi-Steppers. She's not really someone I want to keep hanging with."

"What about Sascha, though? You're cool with her, and she's in PGP. She'll tell my mom about you stealing her boyfriend."

"And what will Mama Gwen do about that?"

Do I have to school her on everything? Dang! "Mama Gwen will most certainly not want you dating Chase. She'll take one look at him and you'll be on lockdown to infinity."

"I guess you're right. I'll just see Chase in secret then.

Forget I told you about the whole thing. I'm going to bed."

What in the world? How can I just un-hear something like this? I'm not wired that way. Once something gets in my head, it totally cannot get back out again.

"Listen, I'm tired of always having Gwen and LeRon in my mix because you're up to shadiness. Why can't you just be a model teen like me?"

"Because you're boring, Gia. I'm in high school now! I need to make some memories. Just think how memorable it will be if I get my first kiss from Chase!"

What would be memorable is the girl-fight that would most probably ensue. And since I don't promote teen violence, I cannot support this cause.

"Candy, if you start sneaking and seeing Chase, I'm telling Sascha."

Candy rolls her eyes and turns toward the wall. "Bye, hater."

My mind goes back to Chase's borderline abusive behavior at the state championship. Just because I didn't say anything when I saw it happen to Sascha, doesn't mean I'll keep quiet if it's my sister.

"Trust me on this one, Candy. Chase isn't as nice as he seems."

"That's your hateriffic opinion."

I shake my head. "Well, do what you want. Just don't tell me about it. Because if I know, I'm blabbing. I've told you up front, so don't get all twisted when I follow through."

Candy turns to face me. "Ugh! I see now why Ricky won't kick it with you! You don't know how to have fun."

Puh-lease! I put the capital F in fun. Shoot, I put the U and the N in too. She can bounce with that foolishness.

"Hurting someone else is not fun to me. Sorry, I don't know where you found your definition of fun. It sounds like you got it out of the Valerie Mean Girl's dictionary."

Candy's eyes light up as if she's just remembered something. "Speaking of Valerie, she's got to have a meeting tomorrow at school with her parents, Susan, and Susan's parents."

"How do you know about all this?" I ask.

"Valerie called me, asking if I knew who hacked her Facebook page. She swears she didn't post those pictures."

"I knew it! I knew she didn't do it."

"What? You believe her? I think she's lying. How do you know she didn't do it?"

"Because if Valerie had done it, she wouldn't be calling you to find out who hacked her page. She'd be calling you to figure out a plan on how to get out of trouble."

"Gia, nobody hates Susan more than Valerie."

I tap my chin, in thinking mode again. "You're right. And everyone knows this. But I think we should be thinking deeper here. What does Valerie really have to gain by posting those pictures of Susan?"

Candy pauses for a moment before replying. "I don't know. Revenge, maybe?"

"But this is going to ruin her entire senior year. Whoever did this either hates Valerie or didn't think about prom, graduation, and everything else."

Candy laughs. "Well, half of Longfellow High hates Valerie."

"I know, right. But when we figure out who hates Susan

enough to ruin Valerie's senior year, then we'll know who posted those pictures."

Candy rolls her eyes at me. "So you're about to go Nancy Drew on us, huh?"

"Nancy Drew? Um . . . no, ma'am. Try Chloe off of *Smallville*. She's fly and she always gets the scoop."

"*Smallville?* You are such a geek, Gia."

"I love you more," I reply as I exit the room.

"I've got a list of three suspects," I announce to Ricky and Kevin the next day at lunch.

Ricky laughs. "Suspects for what?"

"Suspects for who posted those pictures of Susan Chiang on the Internet."

Kevin looks confused. "I thought we'd already convicted Valerie of the crime."

"You have, but not me. Until I see Valerie gloating, I won't believe it. I think she's innocent. And I don't believe we should just say that someone is guilty without any proof."

"The proof is that the pictures were posted from Valerie's Facebook account," Kevin states.

"Purely circumstantial. Her page could've been hacked."

Ricky rolls his eyes and pops a ketchup-covered Tater

Tot in his mouth. "Wow, Gia. You're going all power-to-the-people on us."

"Ew, don't talk with your mouth full. That was just gross. But yeah, I'm team Valerie on this one, until someone proves otherwise."

"But the burden of proof is on Valerie," Kevin retorts. "All the evidence so far points to Valerie. So there."

"Boy, don't you 'burden of proof' me. This is not *Law & Order*. I know she didn't do it, and that's all I have to say," I fuss while Ricky giggles.

"Kevin, it looks like you've got her ruffled. You might make a good lawyer one day."

I give them both the hand. "I am soooo not ruffled. Both of y'all can kick rocks as far as I'm concerned."

Ricky's eyebrows lift, nearly touching his hairline. "Really? We can kick rocks? Well, who's gonna plan your little sweet-seventeen birthday party if we do?"

"Umm . . . sweet seventeen? Since when did it get *that* title?"

Kevin answers, "Since you didn't have a sweet sixteen."

"But I don't want a *sweet* anything. I just want a slamming get-together with my peeps. Don't plan nothing that's gonna get you hurt!"

"So that means no pink streamers?" Kevin asks.

I reply in a low growl. "No, Kevin."

"No Tweety balloons?" Ricky can barely control his giggle as he asks this question.

"Don't play, Ricky. I'm *serious!*"

"She's awful mean and bossy to her two best friends who are planning her birthday party," Ricky says.

"Whatev, y'all know what it is."

Hope plops her lunch tray on the table and says, "Oh, my goodness!"

Her face is completely flushed, like she's just run from somewhere or just heard some juicy gossip. Knowing Hope and her non-athletic self, it's definitely some good gossip.

"What's up, Hope?" Ricky asks.

"Valerie's mom and Susan's mom were about to fight in the office!"

I grab Hope's arm and turn her toward me. "Are you kidding me? Dish!"

"Well, they were having a conference and next thing you know, Valerie's mom started screaming something in Spanish. Then I heard she slapped Susan's mother, and Susan's dad had to hold his wife back."

I press my lips together. "I don't believe that. Who is your source?"

"Regina, the office monitor."

Kevin says, "I wonder what was said to make all that go down. I mean, aren't parents supposed to be the example for us?"

"Now we see where Valerie gets it," Ricky comments.

"Oh, and guess what else—Sascha and Chase are breaking up."

"I heard," I reply, totally forgetting until after I open my mouth that Candy told me not to say anything.

Hope frowns. "What do you mean, you heard? How did you hear and I didn't hear? You been holding out on the scoop?"

"Nah, it just slipped out of my mind until you brought it up."

"Well, anyhoo," Hope continues, "I hear Chase is mad that Sascha is in our PGP group and he doesn't want a girlfriend who's a virgin."

Hmmm . . . This doesn't quite add up. Why would he break up with Sascha for being in the purity group, but then ask Candy out? Maybe he thinks Candy's an easier target. This is messed up.

"I saw Sascha earlier," Ricky says, "and she looked like she was about to cry. If y'all are her girls, y'all need to have her back."

"I've got enough projects going on right now," I say. "When I get done with the Valerie dilemma, then I might have time to focus on other stuff."

"What Valerie dilemma?" Hope asks.

Kevin replies for me. "She doesn't think Valerie did the whole Facebook thing."

"It's funny you say that, because Regina said Valerie just kept denying the entire thing. She said Valerie was crying and everything!"

"See! I told y'all she didn't do it."

Ricky says, "Well, that doesn't prove she didn't do it, that just proves she doesn't want to get in trouble for it."

"Well, her mom took her home for the day," Hope continues. "And she told Principal Welborn that if he doesn't let Valerie go to the prom that she's suing the school."

"We'll be so over this by prom time! The pictures didn't even really show anything," Kevin says.

We all stop, take a moment of silence, and stare at Kevin. I know we're all thinking the same thing, like how long did Kevin actually spend gazing at those pictures on his computer screen. Ewww . . . Double ewww . . . Ewww to infinity.

"What?" Kevin asks. "I'm just saying, it wasn't that serious."

Hope says, "We might be over it by prom time, but Susan's mother is definitely not over it. She's threatening to have criminal charges filed against Valerie. She said something about it being a hate crime."

"Why, because she's Asian?" Ricky asks.

Hope replies, "I guess."

Kevin says, "That would be foul if Valerie did that because Susan is Asian!"

I shake my head in disgust. "Valerie didn't do it."

"You might be the only one who believes that," Hope replies.

"And when did you get to be such a Valerie cheerleader?" Ricky asks. "She hasn't been a friend to you, so I don't get it."

"This has nothing to do with being Valerie's friend. This has to do with right and wrong, and it's wrong to accuse someone of something they didn't do."

"Okay," Kevin says, "who are your suspects?"

"Well, at the top of my list is Kelani. She's pretty heated with Valerie right now, over her boyfriend, Chris," I explain. "Plus, she's always on her Sidekick posting stuff on Facebook."

Hope shrugs. "So what! I'm on my Sidekick all the time posting on Facebook, too. Does that make me a suspect?"

"That and the fact that Valerie had you benched on the Hi-Steppers squad and put salt all up in your game when you tried to holler at Ricky."

Ricky winces and Hope's eyes go straight to the floor. I hated to bring that up, but this is an official investigation. What do you mean, who made it official? I did! So all skeletons are out of the closet and all crushes are fair game.

"Hope is one of your suspects?" Kevin asks.

"Well, she is, but she's lowest on the list. Romeo is next."

"Why would Romeo do something like this? Girls do that type of thing!" Ricky says.

"Two words—50 Cent!" I say with much enthusiasm.

After a pause to think about it, my friends nod, because they could soooo see 50 posting some pictures on the Internet. When he's got beef, he's just grimy with his! The gloves come all the way off. And who couldn't see Romeo, with all his referring to himself in the third person, not getting revenge.

Hope says, "Since I'm a suspect, I don't know if I should be contributing to the investigation, but Romeo doesn't seem to have enough motive. Kelani, and even I, have way more things to hate Valerie for."

"Valerie's been holding the fact that Romeo cheated on his English papers over his head for a while. How do we know he wasn't just biding his time and waiting to get her back?" I ask.

Ricky shakes his head. "Who else?"

"Candy is next on the list."

Hope laughs out loud. "Are you kidding? Candy totally idolizes Valerie."

"Not so much. And to nuke the meanest girl in the school would make Candy notorious! And during freshman year, too."

"That's a little far-fetched," Ricky says.

Kevin asks, "Is that your whole list?"

"So far. Jewel almost made the list, but I don't think she's sophisticated enough to pull something like this off."

And by "not sophisticated" I mean . . . ummm . . . intellectually challenged. Let's just say that Jewel won't be landing any academic scholarships.

"What about you?" Hope asks. "Why didn't you make your list of suspects?"

"Duh! Because I know I didn't do it!"

"Well, if you ask me," Hope says, "you are a huge suspect. Valerie spent all of last year pursuing Ricky, and you know you weren't feeling that. Plus you had to spend the entire Hi-Steppers season being cocaptain with her. Who knows what kind of torture she put you through!"

Now it's Hope's turn to get the hand. "First of all, I don't care who tries to hook up with Ricky. That's his business. Second, Valerie is graduating and I'm going to be captain of the Hi-Steppers all by myself next year. You've got nothing! Zero motive!"

Kevin, Ricky, and Hope all burst into laughter. See,

while they're tee-hee-heeing instead of helping me solve the crime, some random Facebook poster is terrorizing the Internet with scandalous pictures.

"I can't stand y'all," I say.

Kevin winks. "We love you more, birthday girl."

★ 12 ★

As promised, Kevin shows up at my house at eight forty-five on Saturday morning for our SAT prep class. The entire family is awake, but we're chilling and having breakfast. Well, we're chilling at least. Gwen has bombarded us with a new creation called corn cakes. They taste like a burnt cornbread with syrup poured all over it.

Yeah, the taste is so much worse than your imagination could ever dream up.

"Who in the world is ringing our doorbell this early?" LeRon asks.

"It's Kevin," I sigh. "He warned me that he'd be here this early, but I told him not to come."

Gwen says, "Well, get up and let the boy in. It's cold outside."

Candy excuses herself to answer the door when I make absolutely no move to do so. I told him not to get here this early. It is a clear violation of the terms of friendship, plus I'm still mad at him, Ricky, and Hope for trying to clown me in the cafeteria. Especially Hope. She went extra low by almost bringing up my crush on Ricky. She knows that is a "no discuss" topic.

"So where are you two off to?" LeRon asks.

"Kevin and I have an SAT prep class this morning. It's actually every Saturday for the next six weeks. He's taking me over to Mr. Cranford's house later."

LeRon raises an eyebrow. "It's just the two of you? No Hope or Ricky?"

"Nope, just us geeks."

Why is LeRon looking like he's considering not letting me go? That would be an insult beyond insults. Number one—the complete lack of trust, and number two—eww!!! How could he think that anything could be going on with Kevin other than schoolwork? I mean, Kev's made some upgrades of a serious nature, but not enough to erase the vision of Kevin's past from my brain.

"Good morning, Ferguson and Stokes family!" Kevin beams. "What are y'all eating? Corn cakes?"

Gwen smiles. "We sure are! Would you like one?"

"Sure!"

I'm shocked that Kevin has recognized the hard, yellow frisbees as corn cakes, and doubly shocked that he asked to eat one when he knows about Gwen's lack of cooking skills. He better not be trying to sue someone when he gets a food-borne illness.

Kevin sits down at the table and forks a whole stack of Gwen's corn cakes. He must be feeling hungry!

"Did Mother Witherspoon feed you this morning?" Candy asks.

"Yes, but she made oatmeal. I love corn cakes!"

"Well, then eat up while they're still hot," Gwen says.

Kevin takes a bite and chews slowly. Very slowly. I cover my mouth to keep the laugh from escaping. That's what he gets for coming up in other people's houses acting all greedy. He closes his eyes to swallow, and I almost completely lose it.

"Is it okay, Kevin?" my mom asks. "Some of them didn't get cooked in the middle, but they were burned on the edges, so I took them out of the pan."

"They're fine, Sister Ferguson," Kevin replies after one last swallow.

"So, Kevin, do I have to worry about you trying anything fresh with Gia on the way to the SAT class?" LeRon asks all nonchalantly, like he didn't just say the most ridiculous thing on the planet.

"Excuse me, sir?" Kevin asks, his eyes blinking rapidly.

"Well, Sister Gwen and I have a rule that there is no one-on-one dating allowed, and I don't know if we should bend the rules this one time."

My mom, Candy, and I are all staring at LeRon, trying to figure out if he's serious. He's sitting there with a serious, fatherly look on his face. And dang if Kevin doesn't look scared out of his mind!

"LeRon . . ." Gwen says.

Then LeRon bursts into laughter. "Sorry, Kevin. I was practicing. Was I menacing enough?"

"Yes, sir," Kevin says.

If I do say so myself, I think that was kind of rude to Kevin. I mean, in all honesty, we could've been sneaking on a date. If hell was frozen and pigs were flying. I'm just saying.

"Did Kevin tell you that he and Ricky are planning a birthday party for Gia?" Candy asks.

I know she wants to steer the topic away from dating, especially since she's got greasy Chase . . . well, giving chase. Whatever! I don't care if it was a bad pun. I have this sickness where I have to use puns if available.

"That's nice of you guys," Gwen says, "but why didn't you ask us to throw your party, Gia? I've never gotten to give you a teenage party."

"It wasn't my idea at all," I reply. "Kevin was trying to give me some kind of crazy sweet-seventeen thing, and I almost had to end his life."

"Well, it sounds like fun. Where's it going to be?"

"Ricky's parents said we could use their basement. They've got a pool table down there and everything," Kevin boasts.

LeRon asks, "Will there be dancing?"

"Sure," Kevin says. "But you and Sister Gwen are welcome to come. There won't be any funny business at a party I'm throwing."

Boo to Kevin on his random usage of "funny business."

"I think we will come," Gwen replies. "Maybe your aunt and uncle will come, too. What do you think, Gia?"

"I don't care."

And that is the absolute truth. I really don't care. Maybe if there was some boy I was trying to sneak off with, I'd care. But currently there is no reason why Gwen can't come to my party and boogie with me on the dance floor. As long as she doesn't start breaking out old-school dances like the Charlie Brown or the Roger Rabbit. And I'm gonna need both of them to say no to the Robot.

"Ooh, LeRon. We're invited to the party. We must be cool!" Gwen squeals with fake enthusiasm.

"I know, right!" LeRon says, joining in on the fun.

Tee-hee. Whatever.

"Kevin, let's go before they start practicing their dance moves."

And at that, LeRon and Gwen jump up from the table and proceed to do the Bump. They get the tight-lipped side eye.

Parents just don't understand.

Later on in the evening, after my fun-filled SAT prep class—yeah, totally being sarcastic—I'm chillaxin' in my bedroom. My down-filled Tweety comforter is feeling extra nice because it's December already!

Yes, I have one of those almost-Christmas birthdays that makes it almost impossible to get decent gifts. But this year, I'm having a par-tay! Two weeks and counting. Woo hoo!

Okay, so it probably won't be that much fun, but I'm gonna get pumped just the same.

I hear the faint knock on my door that signals Candy's presence. She has a talent for knocking just loud enough that you can hear her and it is annoying at the same time.

"What?" I ask, not wanting to exit my chillaxed mode.

"Can I come in? I want to tell you something."

I sigh. "Come in, but make it quick."

She sits down on my bed, like she's cozying up for a long talk. What part of "make it quick" didn't get to her ears?

"So, I saw something tripped out this afternoon."

"I assume you're about to tell me about it, or are we playing twenty questions?"

Candy rolls her eyes. "Halt on the sarcasm, okay? This is serious."

"Okay, then spill it."

"I saw Chase hit Sascha in the Voc-Ed building tunnel."

The tunnel is what connects the Vocational Education building to the main campus. The Voc-Ed building is new and was built way after everything else. All types of stuff pops off in the tunnels. I've heard about people making out, hooking up, and fighting down there. I try to stay out of the tunnels, myself.

"What do you mean, hit?"

"I mean, smacked her hard on her head. She stumbled and almost fell."

My face scrunches into an involuntary frown. "What did she do?"

"She cried hard. And then—here's the tripped out part—he started hugging on her and she hugged him back!"

I sit up in the bed, chillaxation completely ruined. "She hugged him after he hit her? She wasn't running to the principal's office? She was *hugging* him?"

"Yeah, it completely weirded me out."

"Candy, you know we gotta tell someone."

"Unh-uh! That's their business. And don't you start with all that diarrhea of the mouth you've got, either, Gia."

I fold my arms angrily. "Well, I'm at least saying something to her. Maybe she's just waiting for someone to tell her it's okay to walk away from that jerk."

"Maybe she's provoking him."

"You're kidding, right?" I ask.

"Well, he did mention that she would tease him and promise to hook up, but then never follow through. He said he was frustrated."

I close my eyes and shake my head. I try to remember that I'm dealing with a freshman, but there shouldn't be any way she might justify Chase's hitting.

"No one gets to hit you and take their frustration out on you. That's just wrong on every level."

"Are you telling Mama Gwen?"

"I'm gonna talk to Sascha first," I reply. "She's got to know better than to let a boy beat her up."

Doesn't every girl's mother tell her that? Hmmm . . . maybe she doesn't know better.

★13★

"So, you can tell me, Kelani. We're cool. Did you post those pictures of Susan on Facebook?"

Since they're crowding around my locker first thing in the morning, they must want to talk about something!

Kelani rolls her eyes at me, and her giggle-twin Jewel cracks up. Jewel says, "They already busted Valerie for that. It was pretty easy since she used her own Facebook page."

"Everybody keeps saying that," I say, "but I don't think Valerie's that stupid. I think someone wants us to believe it was Valerie."

Kelani says, "You sound like Valerie's mother. She's talking about someone must've hacked into their computer and done it. I'm like, who would go to all that trouble?"

"Someone who really hates Valerie or Susan and doesn't care about hurting the other girl."

"Who hates Susan other than Valerie?" Jewel asks.

"My point, exactly," I say. "That's why I think the intended target was Valerie."

"Whoever the intended target, it's jacked up for Valerie," Kelani says. "They told her she couldn't go to the prom or even cross the stage at graduation. They said they'd mail her a diploma. Not only that, she can't participate in any dances or fun stuff for the rest of the year."

"Wow! All that over some pictures that Susan says are fake?" I ask.

"Susan *says* they're fake, but they look real to me," Jewel replies.

"So answer my question, Kelani. Did you do it?"

"No, Gia. I didn't do it, but if I had done it, what makes you think I'd just confess to you?"

"Because we're girls, and you know I wouldn't play you."

Jewel says, "I don't know, Gia. You've got a reputation for snitching."

"Whatever! I do not!"

"That's not what your sister says," Kelani says.

"Y'all are tripping! I'm crossing you off my suspect list for now, Kelani, but if I get any evidence that leads to you, I'll be back."

"All right, sheriff," Jewel says.

They both burst into laughter that's too spontaneous to be covering any guilt. I think Kelani may not be the culprit. She's definitely not sad about Valerie's situation; in fact, she seems a little happy about it. But that doesn't make her the villain.

"I'll see y'all later," I say. "I've got English this period and Ms. Beckman don't play."

"Bye, Detective Gia!"

They are the opposite of funny. "Y'all keep it up and I'm uninviting you from my birthday party!"

"No, you aren't!" Jewel says.

"Okay, you're right, but chill on the detective stuff. I'm just trying to help out a fellow Hi-Stepper."

Kelani replies, "That's real noble of you, Gia, but trust and believe she wouldn't do the same thing for you!"

"That doesn't matter. It's about right and wrong."

Jewel sucks her teeth. "You're such a goody-goody, Gia. It's sickening. Get some grime about yourself."

Um, hello! Does anyone remember last school year when I snuck out on an unauthorized date with Romeo? That was grimy and the opposite of goody-goody. I've never been more grimy.

I dismiss Stupid Is and Stupid Does and go on to my English class. Ricky and Kevin are already there and so is my other suspect—Romeo.

"Hey, Gia, almost everybody in the junior class is coming to your par-tay!" Kevin announces.

"What part of the game is this? Did you not hear me when I said *small get-together?*"

Ricky replies, "Yes, we heard you, but word of mouth is a monster."

"Is Valerie coming?"

Kevin and Ricky look at each other and shrug.

"Did y'all invite her?"

They look at each other and shrug again.

"I didn't realize y'all was that tight," Ricky says. "I'll invite her if you want."

"Thank you."

Ms. Beckman starts an extra dry lecture on essay writing and how important it is for our future and blahgity, blah, blah. I can't wait for this day to be over.

When Ms. Beckman isn't looking, Ricky whispers, "You wanna go to the mall later and hang?"

"Just the two of us?"

Ricky shrugs. "I guess, unless you want to invite Kevin."

Way to put the ball in my court, Ricky! He is sooo not slick. He knows he's missing Gia quality time.

"Why don't we ask Kev and Hope? That way we can talk more about my party."

Ricky smiles as if he's relieved. "Okay, cool."

He's not going to get off easy like that. If he wants to man up and ask me out on a date, he's going to have to do just that. Of course, with my mom's anti-dating stance, it's not like I can say yes, but all this maybe-I'm-asking, maybe-I'm-not is not the bidness.

After school, Hope and Candy are waiting at my locker as usual. "What's up, y'all?" I ask.

"Are we going to the mall? That's what Kevin said," Candy replies.

"Yeah, you can go, too," I say with a smile, "although you weren't invited."

Sascha joins our little group. "Hey! What's up, PGP?"

Candy and I exchange glances. She seems awful jolly for someone who caught a beatdown from her boyfriend.

"Look at this!" Sascha squeals.

She holds her hand out for us to look at a ring. It looks exactly like the kind of ring a high school boy buys for his crush—cheap.

Hope says, "Wow, Sascha! Chase gave you a promise ring?"

"Yep. We got into a small argument and he just apologized and told me that he wants us to be together forever!"

Candy says, "That's really sweet, Sascha. I'm happy for you."

"You are? I'm surprised, because a friend of mine told me you were all hugged up on Chase during Singers rehearsal."

"Wh-what?"

Sascha smiles. "It's all good, though. I trust Chase and he told me that you were just a freshman crushing on him. A lot of girls are feeling Chase."

Candy opens her mouth to speak and I elbow her in the ribs. I say, "So I guess he's gonna be your escort to the PGP cotillion, huh?"

"Oh, for sure. That is, if I don't drop out of PGP."

Hope gasps. "Why would you drop out? Are you thinking of giving up the goodies?"

"I don't know," Sascha replies. "I know that I love him, and I know we're going to be together forever, so I don't see why not."

"Are you kidding me?" I ask. "What do you mean, you can't see why not? Two words: teenage pregnancy. Hello!"

Hope pleads, "At least wait until after the cotillion. It won't be the same without you there."

"I'll think about it," Sascha says. "There's Chase now. Gotta go, see y'all!"

Hope and I look at Candy and crack up. "Dang! You got busted macking somebody's boyfriend," I say.

Hope adds, "You better be careful with that, Candy! I know some girls that wouldn't just let that fly."

"Whatever! Sascha has got the story wrong," Candy replies. "I wasn't hugged up on Chase, he was hugged up on me. *He* asked *me* out, not the other way around. I wasn't macking on anybody. Didn't have to."

"I guess you just got it like that, huh?" I ask.

"Actually, I do have it like that. I don't have to steal anyone's boyfriend."

I roll my eyes at the sheer diva of it all. "All right then, fly girl. Ricky's probably waiting outside for us now, so let's roll."

"Are you sure you want to let her near Ricky?" Hope asks with glee in her eyes. "He might start uncontrollably macking on her or something."

Gotta love Hope and her random nukes! We give each other a high five and all three of us jog down the hall.

Oh, and yeah, I'm totally not worried at all about Candy sticking her claws into Ricky. That would sooo never happen.

★ 14 ★

"**C**an I have one of your fries, Gia?" Ricky asks.
I roll my eyes and throw a fry at him. We're at the mall food court and I'm trying to enjoy my favorite junk food dinner, a Philly cheese steak and fries with cheese sauce. Normally, I would not mind sharing, but Ricky already inhaled all of his food and now he's working on mine too.

Maybe that would be acceptable behavior if he was my boo, but in BFF world, a girl's gotta eat.

"Dang, Gia. Don't be so stingy," Ricky says with a laugh. "One day you're gonna be fat."

I laugh out loud. "I'm about a gazillion fries away from obesity, my dude."

He reaches for another fry and I slap his hand. "Can someone loan Ricky three dollars so he can get some more fries for his greedy self?" I ask.

"I just want one of yours, not a whole thing of them."

"But since you aren't getting any more of mine you need to hustle yourself on up to the line and place your order."

Hope giggles. "Y'all fight like two married people."

"My dad and Mama Gwen don't fight like this," Candy says.

Ricky narrows his eyes at me. "All right then, Gia. Be like that. The girl at the counter is a hottie anyway. Maybe I'll get her number."

"Knock yourself out, boo! Maybe she'll give you some free fries!"

Ricky swaggers himself over to the counter and the rest of my friends stare me down. Did I mention how cute Ricky is looking today? His haircut is fresh, sweater is fitted, and the faded brown jeans are off the chain. That girl most probably will give him her number. And I'll most probably be mad, but I won't admit it to anyone but you, so keep your trap shut!

"Dang, will y'all just go together for heaven's sake?" Kevin asks. "I'm sick of the suspense."

"What kind of suspense?" Candy asks.

"All while we're planning Gia's party, he's asking me if I think Gia likes him for real. I'm like, dude! She *likes* you, man. Why wouldn't she like you?"

I lean forward in my chair and drop my fry. "He asked you that for real?"

"Yeah, and I know I'm breaking all kind of man law and friendship codes telling you this, but I'm sick of you two."

Hope grins. "So, Gia, what are you gonna do about it?"

"I'm not doing anything! My mom told me that the boy is supposed to make the first move."

"Technically, he made the first move when he bought you that bracelet," Candy says.

"Nah, because he said that he and his mother picked it out. Even if she did help him, it would only be a first move if he claimed he chose it all by himself."

Hope shakes her head with frustration. "There she goes, making up random rules."

"I know, right!" Candy exclaims. "That was totally random. And this is about to be, too: Kevin, will you be my escort for the cotillion?"

"Seriously?"

"Yeah, seriously. You're kinda cute, and this is a church thing and all, so yeah."

Kevin's smile touches both of his ears. Oh, brother. "Thank you, Candy! Of course, I'll be your escort. What color are we wearing?"

Candy laughs. "Dang, Kevin, it's not the prom. All of the ladies are wearing white dresses, and Mama Gwen says you'll need a tux."

"You already told my mom you were asking Kevin?" I ask.

"Yep. She was cool with it. Who are you asking, Hope?"

"Brother Bryan."

"Brother Bryan, the choir director?" I ask, a little bit salty I didn't think of him first. He's super duper fine.

"Yes," Hope replies. "My mom says it doesn't have to be a boy, but it could be a man that we admire, like an uncle or cousin. I really admire Brother Bryan and he mentors us."

Candy and I give Hope the serious blank stare. "All right!" she says. "He's ridiculously cute, too!"

"The real reason comes out!" I say.

Ricky drops his tray on the table and plops into his seat. "The real reason for what?"

"For why Hope asked Brother Bryan to be her escort to the PGP cotillion."

Ricky scrunches up his nose. "I don't think Brother Bryan is gonna go on a date with a little girl, much less the pastor's daughter."

"First of all, I'm not a little girl! Second, it's not a date! He's just escorting me. Anyway, who are *you* asking, Gia?"

I shrug, even though everybody at the table knows that I want Ricky to be my escort. I hate being set up like this. I'll ask him when I get ready, if I get ready.

"Gia, you want me to take you?" Ricky asks.

Or, I'll wait until he asks me!

"That would be cool, I guess."

Hope rolls her eyes, and gets up from the table to send a text message. An uncomfortable silence settles on the table, as if Candy and Kevin are expecting something more. But Ricky and I just play it cool and keep munching on our fries.

That's how we do.

"Seriously?" Candy asks. "Y'all get on my nerves."

Candy gets up from the table and marches toward Hope.

"What's wrong with her?" Ricky asks.

I give the clueless shrug. "I have no clue."

My phone buzzes in my purse. "Someone's texting me."

The message on my screen says, Heard you're looking for who really posted Susan's pictures online. It wasn't Valerie, but just drop it. If you know what's good for you.

What in the world? Is someone trying to *threaten* me? I don't roll like that. First of all, how you gonna threaten somebody and you don't even leave your name on the text?

"Who is it?" Ricky asks.

"Somebody tripping. Hold up and let me see whose number it is. Y'all know somebody at 216-447-5511?"

Ricky shakes his head. "No. Call them back."

I press Send on my phone to dial the number. Of course the voice mail comes on, with no greeting, and the box is full so I can't leave a message. Hmmm . . . sounds like I need to revisit the suspect list.

"Somebody just sent me a text saying that Valerie didn't post those pictures," I say. I leave out the part about me leaving it alone, because holla . . . I'm not leaving anything alone!

"Ha! It's probably Valerie trying to get Gia all pumped up to investigate," Kevin says.

"I don't know where to go with my investigation," I say. "Kelani doesn't give me any guilty vibes and my gut tells me that Romeo isn't smart enough to navigate Facebook without a tutor, much less post some pictures."

Kevin laughs. "For someone who used to be completely gone over Romeo, you sure can clown him!"

"I was blinded by the beauty. But nonetheless! I have no suspects! This might end up being an unsolved mystery."

Ricky laughs. "You watch too much TV, Gia!"

How about if someone would man up and be my boo, maybe I'd spend less time watching TV and more time convincing Gwen to let me go out on a date.

How 'bout that?

★ 15 ★

So it's Wednesday—three nights before my birthday party—and I'm wondering how much of Longfellow High is actually going to attend. Because it would be straight catastrophic to throw a party and only five people show up. That's why I was leaning more toward having a get-together. Then, if only my bestie circle was in attendance, it would be all good.

I flag down a lonely looking Valerie in the hallway. She's on straight pariah status right about now. The entire senior class is getting underway with planning the second half of their final year of high school. After winter break (which starts on Friday at 3:00 p.m.—woo hoo!) the seniors will start picking prom dates and all that.

I so cannot wait until senior year.

But Valerie is not joining in on all the fun, because she's been banished from it all. Susan has pretty much recovered. In fact, the boys are chasing her right now because of her "fake" pictures. She's probably got a long list of prom date choices.

"What up, chica?" Valerie asks as she stops at my locker.

"You coming to my birthday party?"

"Over Rick's house, right? Yeah, I'll be there."

"You don't sound too thrilled about it."

Valerie gives me a weak smile. "Gia, you know what it is. My senior year is not supposed to be going down like this."

"I know. But you don't have to let it completely bum you out."

"You're right, but it's crazy, because I didn't even do the stuff they're saying I did."

I lift my eyebrows with interest. "I've been saying that since the beginning. It just didn't sound like something you'd do."

"First of all, I'm hardly ever on Facebook. As a matter of fact, I tried to log in the other day, and the password I have isn't even right."

I grab Valerie's arm because flashbulbs are going off in my brain. "Your password doesn't work?"

"No. And I don't know why, because I wrote it down in the back of my diary."

"Sounds like your page has been hacked. Did you answer any strange e-mails asking for your Facebook ID and password?"

Valerie shakes her head. "Nah. I only open e-mails from people that I know."

"So the hacker had to be someone that has access to your diary. Do you carry it around with you?"

"Um, no! It stays in my room, in my special hiding place. No one knows where it is, but me."

"Hmmm . . . maybe you left yourself logged on at a public terminal by accident. Did you ever check your account at the school library?" I ask.

"Once or twice, I guess. I don't know."

"If you want me to help you save your senior year, then you need to think harder than that."

Valerie grins. "Who said I wanted your help? And why do you want to help me anyway?"

"Righting injustices in the world gives me purpose!" I declare in my Martin Luther King Jr. speech voice.

Valerie bursts into laughter. "Gia, you're crazy. I'm gonna miss you when I go off to college."

"Awww, that's so sweet. Where are you going?"

"I'm hoping to get into Spelman, but with this junk on my school record, I don't know what's gonna happen."

"That's all the more reason we need to solve this."

Valerie gives me a hug and it scares me.

"What was that for?" I ask.

"Because you're the only one who's trying to help me. Even my mom told me to drop it."

"Your mom said to drop it? I thought she was going to sue the school and all that."

"That's what I thought too, then out of the blue she just changed her mind. She keeps saying that it'll all blow over."

I shrug sadly. "That's messed up. But I'll help you as long as you want."

"Thanks."

"Are you coming to the PGP meeting tonight?"

Valerie nods. "Of course! Shoot, the PGP cotillion might be the closest thing I get to a prom. Did you find your escort yet?"

"Um, Ricky asked if he could take me." Why do I feel embarrassed sharing this information with Valerie?

"All right! Look at you two, all BFF turned boyfriend, girlfriend. That's so cute."

I clear my throat anxiously. "We're not boyfriend, girlfriend. We're still just friends."

"Not for long."

Ha! Clearly Valerie doesn't know Ricky. It takes him all day to decide which flavor of Kool-Aid he's going to make. (It's always a cherry/lemonade mix, by the way.)

"I can't believe she's here," Candy says, while motioning to Sascha at the PGP meeting.

I, for one, am glad to see her here. Maybe that means she's decided not to hook up with Chase. Hopefully, it means she broke up with his abusive self. I still haven't told my mom about Sascha's issue yet, because I hope she says something herself. Plus, I'm still tripping that Jewel and Kelani called me a snitch.

I'm not a snitch. Am I?

Anyhoo, now that I think about it, Sascha looks kind of sad. Our meeting won't start for a few more minutes, so I'm going to share some Gia cheer with her.

I plop down in the seat next to Sascha. "Hey, girl! What's up?"

"Nothing, Gia. Absolutely nothing."

Mmmm-kay. This coming from the girl who was just

rocking the promise ring and talking about marrying Chase. Speaking of the promise ring, it's missing from Sascha's finger.

"Where's your ring?" I ask.

Sascha's eyes tear up. "I took it off, because Chase is tripping. I wouldn't have come here tonight, but my mom forced me to come."

"Tripping how?"

"Well . . ."

She doesn't get a chance to finish her sentence, because at that very moment Chase and one of his boys roll up into our meeting. Gwen's face is all kinds of twisted. Chase doesn't know it, but he should be afraid.

Aunt Elena says, "Is there something we can help you all with?"

Chase walks farther inside. "Yes. I'm looking for my girlfriend, Sascha. Is she here?"

I glance over at Sascha and notice that she's sliding down in her chair as if she's trying to disappear.

"Well, this is a closed session, young man," Gwen says with attitude. "So I suggest you call or text her later when we're through."

"Excuse me, ma'am, but she's through anyway. Isn't this the purity class? Well, she's not pure anymore, if you know what I mean."

Chase gives his friend a high five, and Sascha's face turns a deep shade of red.

"He's lying," she whispers through clenched teeth.

Gwen replies, "At any rate, this session is for girls only. You'll have to handle your little drama outside of here."

"All right then," Chase says. "Can you tell her I'm looking for her?"

"I cannot," Gwen says.

Chase and his friend crack up laughing and head for the door. Then Chase turns around. "Sascha, I know you're here. You better come here, girl. You know what's up."

Sascha looks unsure for a moment, but then stands. "I'll be right back, Sister Gwen. Sorry for the disruption."

"No, you won't," Chase says. "We're about to bounce. Tell your little church friends good-bye."

Okay, so Sascha looks super embarrassed right now. I would too, because everyone is whispering and Aunt Elena and my mom are looking extra salty.

I take Sascha's hand and say, "You don't have to go."

She snatches it away quickly, but not fast enough for me not to see the purple bruises all over her wrist. She's wearing long sleeves, but I wonder if there are more.

"She's right, Sascha. Have a seat. We'll call your mother if you want," Aunt Elena says, backing me up.

Sascha shakes her head. "It's okay, really. He just wants to talk to me."

Sascha takes her things and heads to the back of the church. Gwen narrows her eyes, furious. Uh-oh. This looks like a job for Ninja Gwen.

My mom says, "Sascha, sit yourself down. Boy, if you don't get up out of this church right now, I'm gonna make you wish you never walked through the door."

Chase chuckles. "What are you gonna do? You can't put your hands on me. I'm a minor."

"No, but I can do this." My mom takes out her cell phone and dials 911. "Yes, I'm at the church with a group of young women and some thugs have broken into our service."

"Thugs! Man, she's tripping!" Chase says. "Let's roll out."

When they leave, Gwen rushes to the door and locks it. She doesn't look scared, but I know my mother. She was worried that some violence was going to go down, and she most definitely will not leave this situation alone.

Sascha takes her seat next to me, and I notice that she's shaking uncontrollably. I think Mom notices it too, because she looks over at Sascha and shakes her head sadly.

Aunt Elena says, "Ladies, I think we've had enough excitement for the evening. We're going to dismiss you, but please stay inside until your ride is here. Thank you."

Before we're dismissed for good, my mom pulls Sascha to the side. She looks more afraid of my mom than she does of that boy who likes to put his hands on her. Crazy!

Hope crosses over to where I'm sitting and whispers, "What was that about?"

"I don't know, but I hope Sascha didn't give it up to Chase. He's so not worth it."

Hope nods in agreement. "I know, right! When did he turn into a thug? He used to be cute grungy, not scary grungy."

"Maybe he's always been like this, but we just didn't know," Candy suggests as she joins our conversation.

"Aren't you the one who was just crushing on him?" Hope asks.

Candy rolls her eyes. "Get it right. He was crushing on me. But he can forget it now. He's tragically flawed."

All three of us watch as Sascha bursts into tears. We

can't hear what my mom is saying, but it must be deep if she's crying like that. My mom signals for Aunt Elena to come over too. They do their signature tag-team prayer on her.

I hope it works, because this scenario, like Chase, is tragically flawed.

★ 16 ★

"**G**ia, Candy, come here!" my mom calls from the living room in her "we need to talk" voice.

I knew this was going to happen. Sascha's little after-school special has turned into an unnecessary parental speech for me and Candy. Me no likee.

Candy and I file into the living room and sit down on the couch while Mom paces back and forth.

"We need to talk," she finally says.

See. I told you.

"I just feel the need to say something to you two about Sascha's situation."

Candy says, "Okay, Mama Gwen, we're listening."

"First of all, please tell me that neither of you find that Chase attractive."

"I don't," I say, and I'm not about to speak for Candy.

Candy rolls her eyes at me. "I used to until I saw him hitting Sascha. That's not cool."

"So he *does* hit her! I knew it, but she denied it."

Mmm-hmmm. Now who's the snitch. Not that I see a problem with it, though. This is totally a snitch-worthy scenario.

Gwen continues. "Listen, girls. Any boy who puts his hands on you is not worth it. And if he does it once, he'll do it again."

"We know that, Mom. We're not stupid," I say.

Candy interjects, "But girls hit too, Mama Gwen. I think that's wrong too, and then the boy gets in trouble for hitting back."

"It is wrong. No one should be hitting, period. If a boy is getting hit, then he needs to open up his mouth and say something. Is that what's happening with Sascha and Chase?"

Candy shakes her head. "No, I don't think so. I was just talking in general."

Gwen says, "I'm glad the two of you have got your heads on straight. You'll need to have Sascha's back when she breaks up with Chase, even though she's out of PGP."

"Why is she out of PGP?" I ask. "She said that Chase was lying about her not being a virgin."

Gwen nods. "Even still, with sneaking out on dates and lying to her mother, her conduct is not something that we want for PGP."

"That doesn't seem fair," Candy protests.

Gwen adds, "Plus, dating and forgiving an abuser is not a good example for the rest of the girls."

"Who says she's going to take him back? Mom, you and Aunt Elena are jumping to conclusions."

I can tell by the scary look on my mom's face that she is so over Candy and I giving her back talk. But I'm dead serious. This is not fair. They're telling Sascha to do the right thing and leave Chase alone, but then they're punishing her for it too? Not a good look for Mom or Aunt Elena.

"Okay, enough," Gwen says with a tone of finality. "Sascha is not the only girl in the program. We've got everyone else to worry about too."

Candy looks like she wants to say something else. I give her a tiny, almost invisible head shake to let her know she should just drop it. I think we'll be able to talk to my mom and Aunt Elena later, after everything calms down.

And after my birthday party! Hello! No ruinations on my festivities are allowed. I'm not sure if I just made up the word ruination, but it is extremely apropos if I did.

I lay three outfits on my bed for Hope's approval. One is typical Gia, with a vintage camo Tweety, skinny jeans, and army-style jean jacket. The second is kind of a glam Gia outfit: a low-key, pink Baby Phat sweater, knee-length jean skirt, sparkly pink leggings, and white boots. The third outfit is anti-Gia. It's one hundred percent bedazzled and sparkly and, yes, it came from Hope's closet. She couldn't resist.

"Which one?" I ask.

"Don't you think that two hours before your party is a little late to be asking for fashion advice?"

I ignore Hope's question. "Pick one or you are completely useless as a friend."

"Well, you know which one I like the best."

"But help me pick the one that I would rock the best."

Hope twists her mouth to one side in silent deliberation. "I like the Tweety combo, but it's too tomboy for this occasion. I'm picking the pink sweater ensemble."

"That's my fave too," I confess. "I think it goes well with my hair."

Gwen helped me put puffy, curly two-stranded twists all over my head. They're pinned to one side and cascading over my shoulder. Trust, it's hotness to infinity.

"Don't forget to wear your charm bracelet," Hope says.

See, here's the thing. I'm debating on whether or not I should wear it. Does wearing it give Ricky too many props? Will it seem like I'm sweating him? I don't know.

"You *are* wearing it, right?" Hope asks.

I pick up the bracelet and turn it over in my hand. "I guess so."

"Look, Gia, this should be a no-brainer. Ricky throwing this party is totally a crush thing to do. You know that, right?"

"Kinda. But Ricky and Kevin are having the party."

"Okay, seriously, Gia. Ricky's mom made him spend his own money on decorations and food. He spent like two hundred dollars out of his stash."

I snap the bracelet on my wrist. I guess the least I can do is wear Ricky's gift. It's not hurting anything.

When I'm fully dressed, I stand in the mirror admiring myself.

"Gia is hot indeed," I say to my reflection.

Hope groans. "If you start referring to yourself in the third person, I am so disowning you."

"Gia is not worried," I reply.

Hope snatches my oversized Tweety pillow and hurls it at me. She better recognize this is my birthday and I can be a diva if I feel like it!

★ 17 ★

The music is bumping as Hope, Candy, and I step into Ricky's basement. A few early birds (Kevin's band friends) are already here and burning up the dance floor. But it looks like everyone else has decided to be fashionably late.

Sidebar. I don't get that whole late-on-purpose concept. I guess it's supposed to prove that you aren't really pressed about the party. But, for real, most everybody picks out their outfit days in advance of a hot party, and they're totally bummed if they don't get an invite. So, show up on time already!

I just had to get that out of my system.

Kevin notices that we've arrived. "Hey, birthday girl," he says and gives me a hug.

"Where's Ricky?" I ask after scanning the room and not seeing him.

"He's upstairs getting snacks. He'll be down in a sec."

Instead of joining Longfellow High's band on the dance floor, Hope and I take a seat next to the pool table. Candy decides that she wants to dance and Kevin is more than happy to be her partner.

"Do you think your parents are really coming?" Hope asks.

A smile teases the corners of my lips. Gwen is so funny with her threats to crash my party. I heard her on the phone with Ricky's mom, making sure that she would be here chaperoning. Ricky's parents are nowhere near as strict as Gwen, but they've got enough of the parent gene to not allow any foolishness.

Slowly but surely, people start to trickle in. By the time Ricky has transplanted the snacks from upstairs to downstairs, the dance floor is almost full.

"Happy birthday, Gia," Ricky says. Then he surprises me by planting a soft kiss on my cheek. Even though it feels completely innocent, my face doesn't know the difference because I feel myself blush. Hope isn't making it any better, because she's one step away from giggling.

"Cool party, Ricky," I say. "Thank you for having it for me."

"You'd do the same for me, right?"

"Of course!"

One of the rally girls dances over to us and says, "What's up, Ricky? The dance floor is calling you!"

Ricky looks at me. "Uh, sure. I guess. Gia, Hope, y'all dancing?"

I wave one hand. "I'm good. Go ahead."

When Ricky leaves with the rally girl to get his groove on, Hope pinches my arm.

"Ow!"

"What was that, Gia?" Hope asks.

"What was what?"

"*I'm good?* Are you kidding me? The boy kisses you and asks you to dance, and you say, 'I'm good'?"

Hope doesn't understand! I've got total noodle legs right now and I still haven't processed Ricky's beyond-BFF-status kiss. I couldn't make it to the dance floor, so forget about dancing. It would not be pretty.

"Well, sit here looking crazy if you want to," Hope says. "I'm going to dance with James. He's looking real nice tonight."

"Okay, have fun."

A few seconds after Hope's ungraceful exit, Valerie takes up residence in her seat. I mean, seriously, can Gia get some alone time? Dang. (Okay, I promise that will be the last time I refer to myself in third person . . . it's addictive.)

"Happy birthday, Hi-Stepper," Valerie says.

"Thanks. Where's my gift?"

"I *came* to your party, Gia. Isn't that enough?"

Valerie's foolishness is a welcome distraction. She's totally making me forget about Ricky's kiss and my noodle legs.

"Thanks for coming, Valerie."

"You're welcome. Act grateful for a change, chica."

Valerie and I share a laugh for a moment. Then she turns serious.

"Gia, I think I know who posted the pictures on Facebook."

Somebody needs to explain to Valerie that my birthday party is not the time to discuss her random drama. Even though my birthday isn't actually until tomorrow, it's *still* my night. Valerie stays putting the spotlight on herself.

I mean, can Gia get a close up? (Okay, for real. *That* was the last time.)

"Who, Valerie? Who did it?" I hope my tone displays every bit of the irritation that I'm feeling.

"I think it was my mom."

My eyes have got to be bugging out of my head. "Are you serious? Your mom? How do you know?"

"She was telling one of her sisters how she 'took care' of Susan, and I was thinking, *what?*"

"And? Took care of her how?"

"Well, I booted up my mom's computer and looked in her picture folder. The pics that were supposedly Susan were in the folder, but they had some other girl's face on them," Valerie explains.

"Your mom Photoshopped some pictures?"

"I know my mom doesn't know anything about Photoshop. She must've paid someone to do it."

"But why? Why didn't she just start her own Facebook page?"

"I thought about that," Valerie replies. "Maybe because most of my friends on Facebook only accept friend requests from people they know . . ."

". . . and she wanted to make sure all your friends saw it," I say, finishing Valerie's sentence.

"I guess so," Valerie says.

"So what are you gonna do? You gonna snitch on your own mama?"

"Naw, chica. Never that. My mami has my back, regardless."

"But what about the prom and graduation?"

Valerie shrugs. "I'm just gonna have to chalk it, I guess."

"That's a craptastrophe, Valerie! Man!"

"Craptastrophe? There you go, chica. Always making up words."

"Nuh-uh, that's on the SAT list!"

I guess I'm looking so serious that she doesn't know whether to believe me or not. I love messing with Valerie. She's so *easy!*

"I'm joking you, Val. It's not really a word."

"Don't play like that, Gia. I'm already gonna have a tough enough time getting into college!"

"Word. I'm putting you on my mama's prayer list."

Valerie laughs. "Does it work?"

"Well, she'd been praying for a husband and she finally got one. So I'm thinking maybe."

Valerie replies, "Then why don't you put yourself on there and pray for some chemicals to fall into your hair?"

"Ha, ha, Valerie. I did used to pray for a relaxer, but God has shown me the error of my ways. Now I embrace the nap-fabulousness that is moi. Deal with it or kick rocks."

"Gia, you are super funny. You should be on that show on BET. The one with the comedians. I think it's called *Who's Got Jokes.*"

Hmmm . . . I can see that. First of all, Bill Bellamy is the truth! He's kinda old, but he's still rocking a little fineness.

Ricky interrupts my television fantasy. "Gia, will you dance with me?"

I smile up at Ricky, because he finally figured out how to ask a girl to dance. But then I panic because it's a slow song. Alicia Keys's "Like You'll Never See Me Again" is coming from the speakers and Ricky is taking my hand.

It's like I'm in a daze, but I feel Ricky put my hand on his shoulder and he puts one of his hands on my waist. Then he grabs my other hand just like we're about to couple skate. Okay, maybe I can make it through the song if I think of it like that. We've couple skated a million times. But not since he gave me the Tweety bracelet and then put his chap-free lips on my face.

Oh. My. God.

For a second I think it's my hand that's trembling uncontrollably, but then I realize that it's Ricky's hand doing the shaking. Then, I get it. He's just as nervous as I am.

I give his hand a squeeze to let him know that it's okay.

I mean, even though we're slow dancing, and that's completely outside of BFF parameters, Ricky is still my bestie. And nothing can change that!

Did I mention that I'm having my first slow dance?

★ 18 ★

I open my eyes and blink a few times. Oh right, it's Sunday morning, my seventeenth birthday. And the day after the best birthday party ever!

Was it all a dream? Ricky kissing me and asking me to slow dance with him! Wow. It still doesn't seem real.

There's a knock on my door and I realize that it's time for the Stokes family tradition. I guess it's going to be the Stokes-Ferguson tradition now, since we're a blended family and everything.

"Happy Birthday to ya!" My mom bursts into the room singing the Stevie Wonder version of the happy birthday song.

If you haven't heard of this version, Google it. I haven't got time to educate you on this right now. I've got birthday presents to open, you know what I mean?

Candy and LeRon follow Gwen into the room carrying boxes. My gifts!

"Thank you! Now hand over the loot!" I say.

I open the first gift and it's from Candy. It's a little Juicy Couture purse. I lift my eyebrows all the way up and so does my mom. Has Candy gone back over to the shoplifting dark side just to get me a birthday gift?

Candy sucks her teeth. "Are you kidding me? I bought it on eBay. Don't be too rough on it. The Juicy logo might fall off."

Everyone laughs out loud at this. Candy done bought me a fake purse off of eBay. Jesus be a fence all around me.

"Open mine," my mom says.

I open the box and it's a digital camera. It's one of the good ones too. I can make movies with this and everything.

"Cool! Thank you, Mom!"

LeRon hands me his box last. I clap and squeal when I see his gift. It's the iPod Shuffle that I've been nagging my mom for since it came out.

"Thank you, LeRon!"

I jump up and give him a hug, which I don't think he expects at all. He stumbles back a little bit but smiles anyway. Hey, it's my birthday. I'm in a great mood.

"After church, we're going out to dinner," my mother says. "Your aunt, uncle, Hope, Ricky and his parents, and Kevin are all coming too. Your pick, Gia. Where are we eating?"

"Cheesecake Factory!"

"Sweet!" Candy shouts and high-fives me.

When we get to church, Ricky pulls me away from my family and into the church foyer.

"Happy real birthday, Gia," he says as he hands me a little box.

"Ricky, you didn't have to get me anything. You threw the party."

He puts his hand up. "Shh! Just don't be looking for a Christmas present. The Gia fund is all tapped out."

"There's a Gia fund?"

Ricky laughs. "There was."

I open the tiny box and inside is a charm for my bracelet. It's a little boot.

"A Hi-Steppers boot?" I ask.

Ricky grins. "Yeah!"

"Cool. Thank you, Ricky."

Now it's my turn to make him uncomfortable. I give him a hug and kiss similar to the one he gave me at my party.

"Ooh, I'm telling! Y'all kissing at church!"

Grrr! This is Kevin ruining a moment. A perfectly innocent moment, I might add. But Kevin doesn't play about the rules of church. As a matter of fact, he's like the church police.

"Boy, ain't nobody doing nothing!" I fuss. "Ricky was just giving me my birthday present."

"Oh. Well, watch yourselves. The Lord can see you."

I shake my head as Ricky and I burst into laughter. Actually, now that I think about it, I'm glad Kevin came and broke things up, because I had no idea what I was going to say next.

"What did you get me, Kevin?" I ask.

"See, what had happened was . . ."

"How you gonna be a bestie and not give me a birthday gift?"

Kevin laughs. "I'm just playing. Hold on a sec. I'll be right back."

Kevin rushes back into the sanctuary.

"He better hurry up. Service is gonna start soon," I say.

Ricky says, "Before he interrupted, I was going to say that it'll be easy to shop for you now. I'll just get you charms every birthday."

"Well, at some point you're gonna have to buy me a new bracelet, because you're going to run out of room on this one."

"That's gonna take some years."

"I know. But doesn't one of the Fs in BFF mean forever?"

"Umm . . ."

Kevin taps me on the shoulder and saves Ricky from responding.

"Here you go, Gia. Hope you like it."

I take the small, neatly wrapped package from Kevin. The paper is cute—pink with little Tweetys all over. My friends are so thoughtful.

"It's a journal. Thanks, Kev! I was on the last couple of pages on my current one, so this is perfect."

"Last pages? Wow, what are you writing about?" Kevin asks.

"None of your business! Dang, you're nosy."

I press the new journal to my chest and walk away from the boys and into the sanctuary. Hope is sitting in our usual seat and Sascha is visiting. She never visits on a Sunday, so I wonder what's up.

Hope scoots over so that I can slide into the pew, next to her. Service hasn't started yet, so we still have some time to chat.

"Hey, Sascha. You weren't at my birthday party," I say. "What's up with that?"

"Oh, yeah. Well, Chase didn't want to come. He thought your mom was going to be there and he didn't want to run into her."

"So you two are still together?"

Sascha nods. "Gia, I'm staying with him no matter what. I really love him."

"Even if he hurts you and tries to force you to do things that you don't want to do?"

"If we broke up and he started dating someone else, it would kill me, Gia. I don't think I could take that," Sascha says.

The sadness in her eyes makes my heart hurt for her.

"My mom says that love doesn't hurt," Hope offers.

"That's not true," Sascha chokes out between sobs. "It does hurt. Especially when they don't love you back."

Sascha excuses herself and runs to the back of the church toward the ladies' restroom.

"Do you think we should go after her?" Hope whispers as the service is starting.

I shake my head. "No. There's not really much more we can tell her right now. We're the ones telling her to break it off with Chase."

"But she should!" Hope exclaims, grabbing my arm for emphasis. "Wait a minute. Is that a new charm?"

What is this girl? Secret Service? FBI? How is it that her eyes went directly to my charm bracelet? And how is it that I'm now under interrogation? She might as well be shining one of those spotlights in my eyes like they do in the spy movies.

"Yes. It's a new charm. You like?"

"Did Auntie Gwen get it for you?"

I smile knowingly. "Nope. She didn't."

"It was Ricky!" Hope squeals way too loud, especially since the grown-people choir is on their way to the choir stand.

Most of the young people at our church sing in the youth choir, so we call the mass choir that sings almost every Sunday the grown-people choir. Some Sundays Kevin sings with them too, which is funny. Every time he does it we call him gramps for a week. He does not appreciate it. But alas, we don't care.

Hope leans in and whispers, "So did y'all make it official? Do y'all go together yet?"

"No! And I don't know if I want to, either. Look how foolish Sascha is acting. If that's what love looks like, it's not a good look."

"Man, they're crazy, Gia. You and Ricky wouldn't be like that."

"Don't keep saying, 'you and Ricky' like we're a couple. If Gwen hears you say that she'll take my head off."

"Well then, stop denying it. You know that you and Ricky are catching feelings."

Okay. Boo to Hope for sounding like one of those old-school throwback rap songs from when we were babies. Catching feelings? I vote no to revamping retired slang.

"I'm not catching anything, Hope. Just nix the whole boyfriend bit for now. We'll get there when we get there. It seems like you and Kevin want it more than we do."

Mother Cranford keeps cutting her eyes at us. That's

called her evil *be quiet* side eye. I know she's about to start tripping, so I elbow Hope in the ribs.

Hope is so dense that she doesn't get the signal and keeps talking. "It's like we've sat through this movie since the ninth grade, Gia. We want to see the end!"

I poke Hope again and then nod my head toward Mother Cranford, who is now scowling. Why do we always sit near her anyway? Hope smiles sweetly at her and I focus on Pastor Stokes, who is just now getting up to speak.

I know that Kevin, Hope, and even Candy are beyond ready to see Ricky and me move into coupledom. But the way things are creeping along for us, it might not be until the sequel!

★ 19 ★

When I get to school on Monday morning, Valerie is standing next to my locker looking beyond irritated.

"Candy, I'll catch up with you later. Let me holler at Valerie and see what she wants."

"All right then, Gia. Talk to you later."

I walk up and say, "Hey, Valerie. What it do?"

Valerie rolls her eyes and gives me a slight nod. "Gia, I know that you live in silly town ninety-nine percent of the time, but I need you to come back to reality for just a second."

Grouchy much?

My nostrils flare but I hold the sarcasm at bay. "How can I help you today, Valerie? How may I be of service?"

She thrusts a wrinkled-up piece of notebook paper in my face.

"What's this? Your homework?"

"Just open it and read it."

On the paper is a letter to Susan Chiang. It's a pretty nasty note, actually, saying that she should've never won Homecoming Queen because she's ugly and fat. Then it says some super mean things about her race, which I'm not even going to repeat. That's how sick it is.

"Valerie, did you write this?"

She gives me a look of disgust. "No. Of course I didn't write that. Now, ask me where I found it."

"Where?"

"In the trash in my mom's office."

"What? What are you saying?"

"I'm sure my mother wrote this. It's her handwriting."

I feel completely and totally confused. Parents are supposed to be the smart, sensible ones. They're not supposed to do stupid stuff. And writing something like this letter is beyond stupid. Gwen would ground me until infinity for something like this.

"But why?" I ask. "This doesn't make any sense. What is she planning to do with it?"

Valerie makes a snorting sound. "You should be asking what she already did! She posted it on Susan's wall on Facebook."

"What! Did she post it under your profile?"

"No. She has a new one. She's calling herself Derek, but the picture is of my cousin Javier."

"And he's on Susan's friend list?"

"Not anymore. But Javier is cute, so a lot of girls accepted the friend request, not knowing it was my mother."

I shake my head, trying to understand. "Have you actually seen your mom logged on to the computer? How can you be sure it's her and not your cousin?"

"First of all, my cousin can't even speak English. He lives in Puerto Rico. And I've been having my girl Phoebe keep an eye on Susan's page, just in case. When she told me about the crazy post on Susan's page, I searched my mom's office and found the letter in her trash can."

Wow. Valerie's mother needs to watch an episode of *Law & Order* or something. Who would keep evidence in their office?

"You've got to tell someone, Valerie."

Valerie lets out a sad-sounding chuckle. "Seriously, Gia. You want me to snitch on my own mother?"

I bite my lip and try to imagine what I might do if Gwen did something like this. Okay, whatever. My mother would never, ever, do something like this.

"But the stuff that your mom wrote . . . It could really hurt someone, Valerie."

"It's just words," Valerie disagrees. "Sticks and stones, right, chica?"

Valerie crumples the letter in her hand and then tosses it in her bag. She flags down Jewel and Kelani, and even though they look like they don't want to, they wait for her.

Before Valerie leaves she says, "Keep this between us, Gia. Okay?"

"Okay."

I slam my lunch down on the table. Hope, Ricky, and Kevin look up at me as if they're waiting for an explanation.

"Don't ask," I say.

Why did Valerie tell me about her mother stalking Susan on Facebook? Why would she put that burden on me, and then ask me to keep it a secret? That is the opposite of everything that is right! Wrong on every level!

"Okay," Hope says, "since we can't ask Gia what she's spazzing about we can talk about my stuff."

"What stuff?" Kevin asks.

Hope pulls out two photos of dresses. "Which looks better? Lots of ruffles or lots of lace?"

"So, what if someone's mom is doing something that needs to be told to . . . I don't know! The police!" I blurt across the table.

Ricky and Kevin's attention switches from Hope's ugly dresses to me.

"Whose mother, what did they do, and why is it that you always have the scoop about stuff?" Kevin asks.

I run my fingers nervously through my afro. "Trust me, Kev. I wish I didn't have this scoop. This is a scoop I would gladly return to sender."

Ricky touches my hand and I flinch. "Gia, you seem really stressed about this. Maybe you should talk to the school counselor or something."

I let out a long sigh. I know that I can't say anything. Valerie's mom could end up in jail or something and I can't be the one that does that to their family.

Right?

Sascha sits down at our table with a puffy and swollen face. I'm gonna need her to stop bringing her doom and gloominess to our circle of friends. We're generally a happy bunch, you know what I mean? This girl stays on crying mode.

"Hope, please ask your mom if I can come back to PGP. I'm still . . ." Sascha glances at Kevin and Ricky and drops her eyes. "I'm still pure."

"Um, I can ask her, I guess, but she and Aunt Elena seem like they've made up their minds about the whole thing."

Sascha replies tearfully, "I know, but it's not fair. I want to be a part of this. I think it's the only thing . . ."

She pauses and looks at Ricky and Kevin again. I lift an eyebrow at Ricky and try to send him a mental signal that this is an all-girl conversation. No boys allowed.

He gets it (because he *always* gets my signals—BFF, remember?). He says, "Come on, Kev, let's go."

"But . . ."

"Kevin, please," I say.

The boys go join another table full of basketball players and rally girls. Okay, Ricky would pick a table with all of his adoring fans. It's going to be very hard for me to focus on Sascha's drama when a rally girl is giving Ricky a back rub.

"I just *have* to participate in the cotillion," Sascha pleads. "Because if I can't, then there's nothing keeping me from hooking up with Chase . . . and I need something to keep me from hooking up with him. Please!"

Hope and I look at each other and I think we must have the same look on our faces. We've got to help her, right? But Gwen and Aunt Elena have made a decision. I don't know if we can change their minds.

Hope finally speaks. "We'll try, Sascha. It's the most we can promise."

"Thank you."

Hope wraps her arms around Sascha and hugs her tightly.

I say, "You know, Sascha. Even if you can't be in PGP, you don't have to lose your virginity to Chase. It's worth more than a cotillion."

Sascha bursts into tears and cries on Hope's shoulder. Is this what it means to be in a teenage love affair? Am I eventually gonna end up crying like Sascha? Is Ricky gonna flip the script too?

Dang. Too many questions, with no answers . . .

★ 20 ★

It's Friday, and school has just let out, beginning our winter break. I should be pumped. Two weeks out of school, hanging out with my friends, Christmas presents, my grandmother's banana pudding, turkey! All good stuff that I can't get excited about.

"Gal, what you over there daydreaming about?" Mother Cranford asks.

I must be the worst employee on the planet, but Mother Cranford keeps letting me come back. When I am at work, I get plenty of dusting done and fix her snacks. Honestly, I think she just enjoys my company. But who wouldn't enjoy my company? Holla!

"I'm not daydreaming, Mother. I've got two friends with some tough situations and I can't figure out how to help with either of them."

"What kind of tough situations?"

"Mother Cranford, I can't tell you. I'm sworn to secrecy."

"Do these friends go to our church?"

"They visit sometimes, but they're not members."

"Then that means I don't know them or their mamas. You can tell me about it, Gia. Maybe I can help you pray on it."

So I tell Mother Cranford all of the drama. And she listens thoughtfully, without making any comments at first. When I'm done, I sit down on Mother Cranford's plastic-covered couch and wait for her to give me her opinions.

She clears her throat and says, "Well, first of all, that no snitching and no tattling mess don't apply to grown folk. Adults are supposed to have good sense, so you don't have to worry about covering up for nobody's mama."

"That's what I thought too, but it's not just going to hurt my friend's mom, it's going to hurt my friend too."

"It'll probably help your friend more than hurt her."

"Maybe you're right."

Mother Cranford whistles. "Now that other one—well, that is a whole other kind of situation. The devil just done got into the youth. I tell you, when I was coming up, no girl needed a reason to keep her britches up."

"It's different now, Mother. Everybody's dropping britches left and right."

Mother Cranford's eyebrows shoot up. "I sure hope you keeping yours up!"

"Oh, of course! My britches might as well be glued to my body."

"You should tell your mama about this stuff. She can help you sort it all out."

"I thought you were gonna help me pray on it."

"I will, but, baby, I'm getting too old for some of this. Talk to your mama. She still remembers being your age."

See what I'm talking about? Even Mother Cranford isn't trying to touch this mess!

Mother Cranford clicks on the television with her remote control. So I guess our little conversation must be over. Dang! Just plain old dismissed right in the middle of my high stress moment!

"Gia . . ."

"I know, Mother Cranford. Lean Cuisine coming right up."

Kevin shows up at my house at 8:45 a.m. for our last SAT prep class. I feel more than ready to take the test and I think we're going to do the next available test date. Kevin and I have college on lock, ya heard!

I hop into the passenger's side of the car. Immediately I turn the heat on full blast. Kevin be trying to freeze a sista.

"Kevin, it's like two degrees out here. My bones are cold."

Just then, I notice that Kevin looks totally tripped out.

"You okay, Kev?" I ask.

He nods. "Can I ask you a question, Gia?"

"Sure, Kev. What's up?"

"If you didn't like Ricky, would you even consider kicking it with me?"

Oh, no. Where is this coming from and where is this conversation headed? Me don't know if me likee!

"Kevin, why are you asking me this? I do like Ricky, so it's highly irrelevant."

Did I just say that out loud? Wow, that's like a major step, and Kevin is so wrapped up in his personal life that he totally just missed the big reveal.

Kevin sighs. "Okay, so it's not about you. I'm over my Gia crush. I've moved on, so I need Gia the friend's advice."

Excuse me! I had a feeling that Kevin had moved on to more fruitful crush territory, but dang, did he have to put it all like that? Oh, the bluntness.

I reply, "Kevin, you are smart, cute, and loyal. Yeah, I'd holla."

Kevin smiles. "Thank you, Gia. I needed to hear that."

"Who are you going after?"

"Your sister, but I'm not going after her. I just wanted to know if she might be interested, in case I ever do try to go after her."

I sit back in my seat and grin. Kevin and Candy would make a weird and cute couple. They're both super-smart and they both like music. And Candy has been dropping hints about Kevin's cuteness for a minute.

"How could she not be interested?" I ask. "You are an awesome guy."

"I'm glad she thinks that. But can I ask you a question?"

"Yep."

"When are you getting a driver's license?"

I roll my eyes. "Jokes, huh? Shut up and drive."

★ 21 ★

"**M**om, I need to talk to you," I say to Gwen as she cuts out recipes.

She sets her extra-large scissors down. "Sure."

Sidebar. I don't know what my mom thinks she's doing with those recipes. Grandma Stokes always comes from her sister's house in Chicago to cook for us during the Christmas holiday. She brings us presents and cooks. That's what she does—it gives her life meaning.

"Ma, what are you cooking?"

She smiles. "I want to surprise my mama and Aunt Penny by cooking everything this year. I want Mama to just relax."

"But Grandma loves cooking! She's even letting me and Hope help this year."

"Gia, your grandmother is getting older and her arthritis is causing her more pain than she wants to admit. So I'm cooking. You and Hope can help me if you want."

I take a huge swallow. "Is there a plan B?"

My mother slams a recipe down on the table. "Did you come to insult my cooking? I thought you wanted to talk about something."

"Sorry, Mom. I do want to talk."

"Then talk."

"There's no easy way for me to ask this, so I'll just say it. Will you and Aunt Elena please consider letting Sascha Cohen back into the PGP program?"

"We've already made our final decision."

"She came to me and Hope and told us that PGP was the only reason she was keeping her virginity. She seemed desperate about it, actually."

My mom bites her lip thoughtfully. "Well, then she is going to give it up sooner rather than later. It's got to be about more than a cotillion, Gia. We talked about that in class, remember?"

"I do, and I told Sascha that. But I think she's just trying to hold on, Mom."

My mother is quiet for a few long moments. I can tell she's torn about the whole thing. Maybe she's thinking about all the stuff she missed out on when she was pregnant in high school.

She says, "We have to portray a positive image for all of the girls, Gia. I'm sorry."

I shake my head angrily. I didn't think she would budge on this, but I had to try. I don't agree at all, but I guess it doesn't matter what we think, because we're just kids. We don't know anything, right?

I *was* about to tell her about Valerie's mother, but I change my mind. My mom is not being very helpful right now, and I'm sure she would make that whole thing even worse.

I get up from the kitchen table. "Mom, I'm going out with Hope and Ricky."

"Where are you all going?"

"Up to Easter Hill Park. He's teaching me how to drive a little."

Mom smiles. "Ricky is brave."

"He's sick of me bumming rides from him."

"Well, you'll still be bumming rides until you get a car, and the way you sporadically work for Mother Cranford, that's not going to happen anytime soon."

"About that, Mom—now that I'm seventeen, can I please get a real job at the mall? I want to work at the movie theater."

My mom had to know this conversation was coming. I need to make some real cash for senior year! Prom, senior class pictures, our trip—all cost the benjamins.

"Let's see what your SAT scores are, and then we'll decide."

"Okay!" This is not exactly a yes, but it's pretty darn close!

"Wait. Didn't you all sign up for a summer program at the beginning of the school year?"

Man! I totally forgot about the hotness that is the summer enrichment program at Columbia University. It's an outreach program for urban kids, to get them interested in attending an Ivy League school. Ricky, Kevin, and I all signed up, but Hope said there was no way she was spending the summer doing schoolwork.

"We won't hear anything on that until the spring."

Gwen nods. "Okay, so when we find out, then we'll decide on the job."

"Mom! If I go to the program won't I need money in New York City?"

"Your uncle will give you money for that. He'll be proud of you."

My mother has an advanced degree in stalling. I know what this is about anyway. Me getting a real job is just another sign that I'm growing up, and I don't think she can deal. What is she going to do when I get ready to leave for college?

Ricky's horn blares outside. "That's them, Mom. I'll see you later."

I run outside and jump into the front seat. The first thing I notice is that there is only Ricky and no Hope.

"Where's Hope?" I ask.

"She asked me to drop her off at the library."

I can feel my heart racing. "So it's just going to be the two of us?"

He pulls away from the curb. "Yep. Is that cool with you?"

I'm feeling something and it's most definitely not cool. Trying to calm down here. This is Ricky—my homie, my ace. My crush.

This is totally in violation of my mom's rules. No one-on-one dating to her means no alone time with a crush. Period. I know this and still I'm rationalizing with myself. Because, for real, Ricky is not just a crush. He's my best friend who's teaching me to drive.

"Are you all right, Gia?" Ricky asks.

Can he tell that I'm having a severe multisystem failure over here? Dang! I've got to work on that obvious thing I've got going on.

"I'm cool. Why?"

"Well, number one, you didn't answer my first question, and two, you're never this quiet."

"Oh, yeah. It's cool, Ricky. I've just got a lot on my mind."

"Wanna share?"

"I don't think I have to tell you that the following reveals are secrets, but I'm saying it anyway."

Ricky nods. "Okay. My lips are sealed."

Dang! Why'd he have to say something about his lips? Those perfectly shaped unchapped lips that kissed me on my birthday? What part of the game is this?

Okay . . . I am not going to fall to pieces here.

"So Valerie's mom is stalking Susan Chiang on Facebook."

"What! How?" Ricky sounds as shocked as I did when I found out.

"She's posing as a boy and saying horrible things to her."

"What kinds of horrible things?"

"Racist stuff."

Ricky shakes his head. "Y'all have proof that it's her mom?"

"Yeah. The profile pic is of Valerie's cousin Javier, who lives in Puerto Rico and doesn't speak a lick of English, and Valerie found a letter in her mom's trash can that was posted on Facebook."

"You telling somebody?"

I shrug. "Why do I always have to tell? Jewel and Ke-lani say that I'm known for snitching."

"No. You're known for doing the right thing. I admire you for that."

"You do?"

"Yep."

This makes me smile. I'm a total sucker for compliments like this. Most boys say stuff like, "You're fly, ma." But Ricky gets who I am on the inside, and that is so much more important to me.

He pulls into a parking spot in the park and gets out of the car.

"You ready?" he asks. "Let's switch."

The good thing about today's driving lesson is that even though it's cold outside, there's no snow on the ground. We haven't had a good snow since November, so we're due. Since I've been alive I can only think of one time we didn't have a white Christmas.

I move over and get behind the steering wheel and Ricky gets in on the other side. I'm going to conquer my fear and do this.

"Okay, Gia. What's first?"

"Um . . . seat belt."

I lock my seat belt and put both hands on the steering wheel.

"How are your feet positioned?" Ricky asks.

"Left over the brake. Right over the gas."

Ricky's eyes bulge out of the sockets. "Gia. You drive with one foot. Your right. Move the left foot from the pedal."

"So how will I stop?" I ask, with fright dripping from my vocals.

"You'll take your foot off the gas and press the brake," Ricky explains.

Okay, how am I supposed to remember all of this? I have to watch the road, check the mirrors, flick on the turn signal *and* remember to switch my foot? No, ma'am. I will ride the bus, thank you very much.

I unbuckle my seat belt and open the door. "Never mind, Ricky. I'm never gonna learn this."

He laughs. "Come on, Gia. It's not hard. Once you get the hang of it, you won't even think about all this stuff. It'll come naturally."

"That's okay. I'll catch taxis, bum rides, or walk. I'm good."

"Wow, I didn't know that my best friend was a quitter."

Quit? I haven't even started. It doesn't count as quitting if you never begin. Yes, that was a totally random rule. I haven't made up one in a while.

"Not quitting, Ricky. Just postponing. Maybe I'll learn in the spring."

"Just a few feet down the parking lot, Gia. No turns, nothing fancy. Just put the car in drive, gently press the gas, roll a little bit, and then press the brake."

"Well . . ."

"I'm right here, Gia. I won't let you get hurt."

This Ricky 'the protector' person is niiice. I feel my insides getting all gooey at his words.

"Okay."

I close the door and click the seat belt again. This time I'm determined to drive just a little bit. I check the mirrors, take a deep breath and press my foot down on the brake. Then I shift the gear into drive.

Ricky says, "Whenever you're ready, take your foot off the brake and just roll for a second before you step on the gas."

I grip the steering wheel and try to hold my hands steady, but they keep trembling. Very, very slowly, I remove my foot from the brake pedal and the car rolls a little bit.

"Should I press the gas now?" I ask.

"If you're ready."

"Okay."

I take one last deep breath, and press down. Wait! Am I pressing too hard? Why are we going this fast?

"Gia! Ease up!"

"How do I ease up?"

We're running out of parking lot here!

"Take your foot off the gas, but don't . . ."

I take my foot off the gas and slam on the brake pedal. The tires screech and we lurch forward in our seats. I'm glad we are both wearing our seat belts. Safety first.

Ricky exhales. "I was going to say, don't slam on the brake."

"Well, we're stopped now. How did I do?" I think I already know the answer to this question.

"You just need some practice, ma. You'll get it."

I crack a tiny smile. "Are you going to keep teaching me?"

"Yes, but I'm wearing a helmet next time."

"Hahahaha. Jokes!"

★ 22 ★

Hope and I have been at the mall all day, trying to find an appropriate Christmas gift for Ricky. Seriously, what do you buy for your BFF who's almost made it to boo status? Exactly! We don't know either.

"What about a sweater?" I ask.

"No. Too boring. He's not your uncle, Gia."

"Well, then what? Cologne?"

Hope laughs. "No! That's not sentimental enough."

"But I do like it when he smells good."

Hope shakes her head adamantly. "Absolutely not."

"Tennis shoes?"

"My mother says that if you buy a man shoes, then he'll walk right out of your life."

"Are you kidding me? So she's never bought Pastor Stokes a pair of shoes?"

Hope shrugs. "I think that only applies to when you're dating someone."

This is crazy! Boys are too hard. There's a ton of girlie stuff you can buy me. Especially when I love Tweety so much. Ricky has lots of choices.

"I know! You can buy him a giant key and say it's the key to your heart!" Hope squeals this as if it is a great plan.

Gag on top of gag. But then again, this is coming from the girl who writes twenty-page letters in purple ink. What can I expect?

"Hope, there is no way I'm doing something as lame as that. No, ma'am."

"Okay, then just get him that stupid, boring wallet that we saw earlier."

The wallet was not stupid or boring. It was leather and it was nice. Ricky needs a wallet. He's always got his money balled up in his pocket.

Hope asks, "What does Ricky like more than anything else?"

"Sports," I reply.

"So why not get him something sports related?"

I ponder this for a second. "Ricky will look scrumptilicious in a Tennessee Titans jersey."

"Why the Titans? Isn't Ricky a Browns fan?"

"He likes the Titans too, and I just pictured him in that Titans blue and navy blue. Niiiice."

"Ewww, Gia. You are out of control."

"Come on, let's see if they have a good one in Foot Locker. We can get a hat to match at Lids, too."

Hope laughs. "Dang, you're breaking the bank on your little boo, huh. What's everybody else getting?"

I shrug. "Umm . . . let's hit the dollar store before we leave."

Hope bursts into giggles. "Wow!"

We start toward the Foot Locker, which is, of course, at the other end of the mall. On our way over, we see a pack of Longfellow Spartans girls. Mostly rally girls, but some not. Hope waves, and they all rush our way.

"Dang, Hope! You know I'm on a mission," I fuss, not wanting to stop and have girl talk.

"Chill out, Gia. We know what we're getting now. We've been running around here for hours looking at stupid stuff. I need a break."

As the girls approach, I can tell that something isn't right. Sascha is crying. Oh, wow. So not in the mood for a crying girl today, not in the middle of my power shopping.

"Sascha! What's wrong?" Hope runs to her and gives her a hug.

"It's not me!" Sascha wails. "It's Susan. She's in the hospital."

"What?" I ask. "Is she hurt?"

Cecile, another of the rally girls, says, "She took a bunch of pills and wrote her mom a letter saying that she doesn't want to live anymore."

"Why would she do something like that?" Hope asks.

Sascha replies, "Some boy that she met on Facebook told her to do it. She really liked him, and she thought he liked her too. But then he started being really mean and told her that she should have never been born."

All of a sudden my legs are wobbly. I stumble over to

the nearest bench and sit down. They just told me that Susan tried to commit suicide because someone was teasing her on Facebook. And I know that someone is Valerie's mother.

I have to tell someone now. I have no other choice.

I walk back over to the group. "What hospital is Susan in?"

"Lakeside. But she can't have any visitors."

She may not be able to have visitors, but the person I'm telling can go into the hospital any time of the day or night without an invitation.

"Come on, Hope. Let's go get this jersey. Call your dad so he can pick us up. I want to talk to him," I say.

"You sure you don't want to hang with the rally girls for a while, just until everyone is okay?"

I give Hope my most serious glare. "Hope, I need to talk to your dad, like right now. It's an emergency."

Hope gives an apologetic look to her crew. "I'll catch up with y'all later. Gia is tripping."

I walk quickly to Foot Locker, with Hope barely able to keep up. When she finally catches me she says, "What was all that about?"

"I know who the boy is on Facebook."

Hope shakes her head. "No, you don't. It's this guy named Javier, and he doesn't even go to our school."

"I know. He lives in Puerto Rico, actually, and can't speak any English," I reply.

"What? That doesn't make any sense! He posts in English all the time."

"Trust me, I know what I'm talking about, and I need to tell your dad. Pastor Stokes will know what to do."

"It's Valerie, isn't it?"

I shake my head. "Nope. But I can't tell you who."

Hope takes out her cell phone and calls her dad. "Daddy, can you come pick us up from the mall? We've finished shopping for today and Gia wants to talk to you about something . . . Okay, see you in a few . . . Bye, Daddy!"

She looks at me and says, "Okay, my dad is on his way. Satisfied?"

"No, but I will be once I pay for Ricky's jersey."

I look at the selections on the rack and find a perfect one for Ricky. He wears a large, because he likes a little extra room to layer it with a turtleneck or long sleeve T-shirt. How do I know the size? Because I have stolen many of his jerseys to rock with jeans and jean skirts. Yeah, that sounds like a girlfriend kind of thing to do, but I've been swiping Ricky's clothes since middle school, and there was no romance going on then.

Actually, there's no romance going on now, but we're moving in the right direction, I think. He's trying to be my official boy.

Pastor Stokes drops Hope off at home and takes me for ice cream. I love talking to my uncle, because desserts are always involved. He has a sweet tooth and is constantly looking for a good reason to buy something yummy to eat.

We're sitting at the table in the very uncrowded Baskin-Robbins shop. I guess since it is winter time, not too many people are trying to eat ice cream. Pastor has a banana split and I've got a one-scoop sundae.

"So, what's going on, Niecey? What do you want to talk about? Everything okay at home?"

I nod. "Everything is cool. LeRon and Candy are cool, I guess. I think I just had to get used to them."

"Glad to hear that!" he says with a smile. "So what's bothering you then?"

"A girl in my class tried to commit suicide."

Pastor gasps. "In your class? Is she okay?"

"She's in Lakeside Hospital. She did it because she thinks a boy was being cruel to her on Facebook."

Pastor's eyebrows go up, almost forming a straight line on his forehead. "She *thinks* a boy was being cruel? Was he not being mean to her?"

"Oh, he was being mean, but he isn't really a he."

"Ah. Is there some girl tormenting the young lady?"

I squeeze my eyes tightly shut and scratch my head. I know that once I say this, I can't take it back. And it's going to be all bad for Valerie's mom once I say something.

"It's not a girl, Pastor. It's my friend's mother."

"What! Which friend, Gia?"

"It's Valerie's mom, Mrs. Lopez. She's pretending to be a teenage boy on Facebook."

Pastor shakes his head. "And a young girl tried to kill herself over that?"

"Yes. I'm afraid Valerie's mom won't stop."

"Why would she do something like this?"

I shrug. "First, I think she was angry that Valerie didn't win the Homecoming Queen title. But then, I think she was mad that Mr. and Mrs. Chiang came up to the school and embarrassed her."

"I have never heard anything so crazy in my entire life," Pastor says.

"Valerie is going to be so mad at me. I doubt she'll want to be friends with me anymore once this comes out."

Pastor sighs. "Gia, do you think that Valerie or her mother wanted someone to die over this?"

"No, I hope not."

"Well, then they have to know that this has gotten totally out of control. Don't worry. I'm going to call up to the hospital and talk to the Chiangs. I won't even bring your name up."

"Thank you, Pastor."

I feel relief rush over me like a wave at the beach. Not one of the tiny ones that just tickle your toes, I'm talking the wave that picks you up off the ground and throws you onto the sand.

Yeah, super relieved.

Because I know that my uncle is not going to drop this, and he's going to do the right thing. I kinda feel like it's my fault that it went this far, because maybe I should've told my uncle from the jump.

"Is there anything else you want to tell me?" Pastor Stokes asks.

I take a very long pause. Should I mention the whole Sascha thing? I think my mom would completely flip out if I go over her head to my uncle to get Sascha back into PGP. But she and my aunt are not listening to reason. Hmmm . . . I think I'll wait to ask him about this. He'll be my last resort.

"Umm . . . that I want an iTunes gift card for Christmas?"

He smiles. "You kids and those little iPods! I'll get you a gift card if you promise to only download gospel songs."

I scrunch up my nose. "How about if I download one gospel song."

"Deal. You drive a hard bargain, Gia."

I give my uncle a fist pound. "Thank you, sir. Good doing business with you!"

★ 23 ★

I've just finished wrapping Ricky's Christmas gift with my shiny, cartoon-print wrapping paper. I actually wrapped everything, and no, I did not get everyone else's gifts at the dollar store.

I got Hope and Candy cute House of Deréon baby tees. I bought my mom a cookbook. No explanation needed. For LeRon, I got a slamming tie at Macy's. His selection is pretty old-school, so I scored him a DKNY tie on sale. Kevin gets a copy of *Eragon*. He's gonna love it.

My phone buzzes on my hip. "What it do?"

"Hey, you."

An involuntary smile pops up on my face. It's Ricky. "Hey. What are you doing?"

"Watching TV. You?"

"Just got finished wrapping gifts."

"We going over to Pastor Stokes's house?"

Everyone always goes to my uncle's house on Christmas.

The entire day, members of our church stop in and say hello to the family. Sometimes they bring gifts for Pastor and Aunt Elena. Some of them stay and have a plate of food. Grandma Stokes usually cooks enough for everyone. I'm sure with my mom doing the honors this year, there won't be too many people sticking around.

The young people all chill in Pastor's basement, playing pool and exchanging gifts. It's like our own little youth ministry Christmas party. It's the one time all year that no one has a curfew.

"You know I'm going over there. I'm helping Gwen cook this year."

Ricky laughs. "You in the kitchen? What are you making? The water?"

"You're such a comedian. Hope is helping too. My mom is doing most of it."

"Aw, man. Sister Gwen burns hot dogs. She can't be cooking the Christmas dinner."

"We tried to tell her, but she's determined to show Aunt Penny that she can do it. I think my grandmother will be there to oversee, so it shouldn't be too bad."

I can't believe Ricky brought up the burnt hot dogs. One time when we were little, my mom made us eat these hot dogs that she boiled until all the water left the pan. She tried to convince us that they were barbequed outside. We were ten, but we weren't stupid. That had to have been the nastiest hot dog I've ever eaten.

"What did you get me for Christmas?" Ricky asks.

"You'll find out when you open it."

"Is it good? Am I gonna like it?"

I laugh out loud. "Dang, Ricky. You're worse than a little kid. But to answer your questions, yes and yes."

"Sweet! I can't wait."

"Ricky, I told Pastor about Valerie's mom."

There's silence on the line for a moment. "You did? Why?"

"You heard about Susan, right?"

"Oh, yeah, that's messed up. I overheard my mom on the phone talking about it."

"Well, that's why I told. I couldn't keep the secret anymore after that. If Valerie is mad, then oh, well."

"I know that's right."

Both of us are quiet now, but I don't think that he wants to get off the phone. I know that I don't. It's a good thing it's evening, or my mom would flip out if she knew I was using daytime minutes on my cell phone to listen to Ricky breathe.

"You ready to go driving again?" Ricky asks.

"Not yet."

Ricky laughs. "I had fun that day, Gia. You were so scared."

"How is it that me being scared equals fun for you? I don't get that."

"I just like being with you period, Gia. So that's why it was fun."

Gulp. I hate when Ricky does this. He'll just spring some random boyfriend-like sentiment on me when I'm not ready. He likes *being with me*? How do I even respond to that without sounding totally foolish?

Maybe I shouldn't care how I sound.

"Yeah, it was kinda fun, I guess."

Yes, I know this was a total cop-out, but I'm not ready to go there yet. Because what if when I get there, I start acting stupid like Sascha? What if I start saying ridiculous stuff like, "I would die if he's not with me." Dude! Totally not trying to go there, and yet it seems inevitable that teenage love goes there.

"You talked to Chase lately?" I ask, trying to change the subject.

"Nah. He and I aren't that cool, especially since he started putting his hands on girls. That's not cool."

"Sascha is still trying to be a part of the PGP cotillion, but my mom and Aunt Elena aren't trying to hear it."

"Did she break the rules?" Ricky asks.

"That's the thing! She didn't break the rules at all. They just don't like the idea of a girl who has an abusive boyfriend being one of the debutantes."

"That sounds like Sister Gwen. You've already tried to talk to her, I guess."

"Yep. She's being completely irrational about the whole thing. She won't even hear me out anymore."

"That's messed up. Do you and Kev know the date for your SAT test yet?" Ricky asks.

"Yes. We go on January twelfth. You can go too, if you want. The deadline to sign up is the day after Christmas."

I can't believe we're taking the SATs! We're almost seniors. It feels like high school has just gone by way too quickly. One day we were pimply, skinny little freshmen and now we're almost grown. It's just crazy. I guess I understand how my mom feels about me growing up.

We're quiet again, but like I said before, the quiet is cool.
I feel my eyelids getting heavy, so I know that I'm gonna
be asleep in a few minutes.

"Ricky, I'm falling asleep. Do you want to just talk tomorrow?"

"Okay, but you hang up first."

Seriously??? I can't stop smiling. "No, you first."

Ricky laughs. "Okay, on three. One . . . two . . . three . . ."

We both burst into laughter because neither one of us
hangs up.

"Good night, Gia."

"'Night."

"Merry Christmas! Wake up, Gia!"
What is the meaning of Candy hovering over my bed at the crack of dawn like she just saw Santa Claus fly up the chimney? We are not three years old and I need my beauty sleep. I'm seeing Ricky today and I can't be all puffy-eyed and grumpy.

I'm just glad Christmas morning didn't fall on a Sunday this year. Pastor Stokes always gets ridiculous with calling for a sunrise service when a holiday falls on Sunday. The choir always sounds a hot mess on these days. Sopranos sounding like tenors—everybody singing in their hot morning-breath voices. Trust. All bad.

"I'm not awake, Candy. Come back in a few hours."

"It's Christmas! Don't you want to open your gifts?"

Well, I'm awake now so I might as well get up. "All right. I'm up."

"You want to make breakfast?" Candy asks.

She's way too gleeful for it to still be dark outside. And she has on antlers. Why is she wearing antlers? That is just unnecessary and I'm almost sure it's against some rule somewhere.

"Yes, how about some bowls of cereal."

"Don't be a grinch, Gia. Let's do pancakes."

"Are you kidding me? I'm not trying to make pancakes."

Candy leans on the counter and takes a deep breath. "Okay, Gia. I'm only going to say this one time, so listen up. My mom made pancakes with me every Christmas morning, until last year when she decided that *her* life was more important than me. So, just chill and make the pancakes, okay? I need this."

"All right then, pancakes."

We go into the kitchen where it looks like there's already something going on. My mom has piles of neatly stacked recipes on the counter and when I open the refrigerator, ingredients are lined up in some kind of order. There are little sticky notes with numbers and letters on them.

"Hand me the milk," Candy says.

"Umm . . . it has a number two and an M on it. What do you think that means?"

"It means that's the second thing I'm cooking and the M is for macaroni and cheese," my mom says. "Drop the food girls, I've got a system going on here."

"Well, we want to make some pancakes for breakfast," Candy whines.

"You all better get a piece of toast and get up out of my kitchen unless you're planning to help."

Candy replies, "Excuse me! I thought we were helping by making breakfast."

"It really doesn't make any difference to me," I say. "I'm not hungry, so I don't need to make any pancakes. I was doing that for Candy."

"I will need you two in a little while, once we get over to your uncle Robert's house. I'm doing the majority of the cooking over there."

"Is Grandma here yet?" I ask.

"Yes. Your aunt and uncle went to get Grandma and Aunt Penny from the airport last night."

I hear my phone buzzing in my bedroom. "Someone's calling me."

I dash back into the room just in time to miss the call. It was Hope. I press the Send button to call her right back.

"Merry Christmas!" Hope squeals into my ear.

"Merry Christmas right back at ya. Is Grandma awake yet?"

"Yep, and she's making breakfast—waffles and stuff. Y'all coming early?"

"I don't think my mom is. She's doing something to the turkey. Maybe Ricky will bring me over there."

"If you had your own license you could come on your own," Hope teases.

"Whatever! Did Ricky tell you about our little lesson? I almost perished in that car. No thank you, ma'am. Plus, you don't have yours either, so shut up."

"Well, I don't need mine because the waffles are getting cooked over here," Hope taunts. "Is that blueberries I smell, Grandma?"

I hang up on Hope when she says something about warm, sweet syrup. I'm not trying to hear that, especially since I'm holding a dry piece of wheat bread in my hand. It's not even toasted!

I press the numbers in to call Ricky. "Merry Christmas, Gi-Gi. What it do?"

"Merry Christmas, Ricky Ricardo. You hungry?"

"Famished! Nobody is awake here."

"My grandmother is making waffles over at Pastor Stokes's house. You down?"

"Give me fifteen minutes to get to you and then it's on and popping!"

I laugh out loud. "You are greedy with a capital G."

"Whatever. The only reason you called me was to get a ride to the food."

"You got me. But right now, you're still talking instead of showering. I need to get something on, too."

"See you in a sec."

"Holla."

I poke my head out of my bedroom door and say, "Candy, if you want Grandma Stokes's waffles, be ready in fifteen minutes. Ricky's coming to take us over there."

"But aren't we going to open gifts and stuff?" Candy asks.

My mom interjects, "We usually do that over at my brother's house. You can go if you want."

"Grandma Stokes's waffles are the bomb diggity. Come on and get dressed. If you aren't ready by the time Ricky gets here we're leaving you."

Fifteen minutes later, Candy and I are dashing out the door. On my way out, I notice that my mom is doing something totally inhumane to that turkey. Well, it would be inhumane if the turkey were still living, but since it's about to be dinner . . .

"Mom, are you okay? Do you need any help?"

My mother pulls her arm out of the turkey's behind and waves a little packet in the air. "Got it!"

"Mom?"

"No, Gia. I'm fine. Why don't you and Candy pack our gifts into Ricky's car so that LeRon and I don't have to."

I wave for Ricky to come in, so that he can help. Why? Because I try not to lift too many heavy boxes when there are boys around. I'm all for girl power, but they like carrying stuff. It makes them feel good.

Ricky steps inside as Hope and I gather the boxes and put them by the door. He's looking extra nice with his thick brown leather coat and Timberland boots. Even this early in the morning, his caramel skin and big brown eyes are looking real nice.

He completely and totally shocks me by giving me a big hug. "Merry Christmas!"

"Merry Christmas, Ricky!" Candy says, giving Ricky a hug too.

I'm sooo glad Candy did that, because I could feel my mother's antennae go up when Ricky spun me around the room. She's got to see how fine Ricky is looking right now, so if she hasn't already suspected some crushing, she probably will now.

"Merry Christmas, Sister Gwen!" Ricky says. "That turkey looks like it's met its match."

"Hey Ricky, Merry Christmas," Mom replies with a little giggle.

She sounds like she's having fun, so even if the turkey

ends up burnt and dry, I guess it will have been worth it.
But I'm really hoping for a Christmas miracle like in one
of those family movies they always show on the holiday.
Maybe someone will sprinkle some kind of dust on my
mom when she starts cooking!

Ricky grabs a pile of presents and heads out the door. I
try to hurry behind him, because I don't want to answer
any of the unspoken questions that I see on my mom's face.
But y'all know how Gwen does.

"Candy, you go on and help Ricky. I want to talk to
Ms. Gia for a minute."

Aw, dang. Why I gotta be Ms. Gia? That means that
she's tripping on something.

"What's up with you and Ricky?" Gwen asks as soon
as they're out of the house.

"Nothing's up. Why do you ask?"

My mom narrows her eyes. "If nothing's up, then why
can't you look at me? He's got a little crush, doesn't he?"

I shrug. "I don't know. Maybe."

"What about you? You have a crush too?"

Again, I shrug. "We're best friends, Mom."

"Well, best friends or not, I need to keep an eye on you
two," my mom says. "You all aren't babies anymore, and
Ricky is turning out to be a little hottie."

The smile creeps up on me before I can stop it. My
mom continues. "See! I knew you thought he was cute.
Go on over to your uncle's house."

"Okay."

"Just remember, I'm watching you."

"Yes, Mom. I know."

*   *   *

I'm so happy to see my grandmother and Aunt Penny. They haven't visited since my mom and LeRon got married, and they live all the way in St. Louis, Missouri. Grandma went to live with Aunt Penny a few years ago when she got too sick to live alone.

I give my grandmother a gigantic hug. "Grandma Stokes! You're here!"

"Yes, baby, I'm here! Candy, come give your grandmother a hug."

A huge smile beams from Candy's face. I think she wondered if she'd be accepted as family during a Stokes Christmas, but everyone is family to my grandmother. She's cool like that. Candy wraps her arms around my grandmother's neck and hangs on for dear life.

"And is that Ricky Freeman?" Grandma Stokes asks. "Boy, you are getting more and more handsome every time I see you."

Aunt Penny chimes in, "Gia, you better snag him before someone else does."

I roll my eyes. "You two are going to give him a big head with all that."

"I'm serious!" Aunt Penny says. "If you were about ten years older, I'd give you my number."

Ricky is completely embarrassed now, and his face is a hilarious shade of red. He scratches the back of his head and says, "Didn't someone say there were waffles here? I'm hungry."

The aroma of the waffles floats in from the kitchen. It smells like those funnel cakes that you get at the amusement park. You know how you can smell the sugar rising up off of them. Grandma Stokes can put the mack on some waffles.

Candy asks, "Can we eat? They smell so good."

"Help yourself, baby!" Grandma Stokes says.

Aunt Penny adds, "Y'all better get full too, because it might be the only decent meal y'all get all day long."

Pastor Stokes comes in from the den. "Penny, don't start. Gwen is working really hard on the dinner, and when she brings the food over here, we're all going to help. Isn't that right, girls?"

Candy and I nod. Where is the third kitchen helper? While we're out here agreeing to be my mom's kitchen guinea pigs, Hope is sitting at a bar stool in the kitchen, stuffing a syrup-soaked waffle down her throat. Just plain old greedy.

Candy, Ricky, and I take off our coats, wash our hands, and dig into the breakfast buffet my grandmother has prepared. I don't know what my mom is talking about. Grandma Stokes doesn't seem sick at all, and whatever is bothering her sure didn't stop her from making a slamming breakfast.

"When is your mother coming over here with that husband of hers?" Aunt Penny asks.

"I don't know. I think she was prepping the turkey and then they were coming."

Penny laughs. "I guarantee you that Gwen knows nothing about prepping a turkey. Why didn't she just bring it over here?"

"Now, Penny, we're not having any mess outta you and Gwen today," Grandma Stokes says as she walks slowly back into the kitchen. "You're a good cook, so give your sister a hand. This is the day we celebrate the birth of the Lord. I don't want no mess."

Well, Grandma Stokes done laid down the law. They better listen up too, because I think my grandmother is not above taking her cane to one of them. Actually, it might be funny to see my mom getting a beat-down. It might be something for the record books.

Hope says, "Bring your plates downstairs so we can open our gifts."

"But Kevin isn't here yet," Ricky objects.

"Yes he is! He's downstairs on Daddy's couch taking a nap. Y'all know Kevin is always the first one here. Deacon and Mother Witherspoon already came to say Merry Christmas."

We take our plates down into the game room, where there is a table already set up with a tablecloth.

"Wake up, Kev!" I shout when I'm close to Kevin's ear.

He sits up straight on the couch and has a hilarious, disoriented look on his face. He's been chilling so hard that he's got couch lines on his cheek. Not a good look.

"Present time!" Hope sings.

She makes little piles of gifts for everyone. We'll open our parents' gifts later, but this is the time when the crew opens gifts. This is Candy's first year, so she's got to learn the rules.

Ricky explains. "Everybody picks a number, and then we go around in order, opening one gift at a time, until everything is opened."

"Cool," Hope says.

Kevin passes around the hat and we pick the numbers.

Great—I'm number five, so I won't get to see Ricky's gift until last. Because of course, I'm opening his gift last. Candy picks the number one.

"I'm opening my sister's gift first," Candy says, "since this is our first Christmas as a family."

Okay, that almost made me get a little emotional. But I'm too fly for that. I give Candy a little wink and nod.

Candy claps her hands together. "A House of Deréon tee! It's cute. Thank you, Gia."

And then she jumps up and kisses me on the cheek. Aw, dang. Didn't expect that, and now I'm losing all kinds of cool points for tearing up. Ack.

Kevin is next and he opens Hope's gift. He holds up a fly Fossil watch that we scored on sale. "Thanks, Hope. That's hot."

Hope opens Ricky's gift first. "Paris Hilton perfume! Yay! You're good, Ricky."

Ricky and I share a glance. The perfume is an inside joke between me and Ricky. We always say that Hope thinks she's a black Paris. But of course, we always say this behind her back.

Ricky opens Kevin's gift, and it's a pair of leather driving gloves. "Good looking out, Kev. I wonder when Gia will need driving gloves?"

"Why the jokes? It's Christmas Day!" I fuss. "I'm opening Candy's gift."

It's a very cute jean miniskirt. It's fresh, but something I'd absolutely never wear. I smile anyway.

"Thank you, Candy!"

"You're welcome. I noticed that there weren't enough minis in your closet. One can never have enough minis."

"Is that so?" I ask.

"Yeah. So once you break it in, I'll borrow it from you. I've got some little pink boots that would look flawless with it."

I chuckle to myself. Isn't it just like a little sister to buy a gift for you that she really wants for herself? It's all good though. I'm not mad at her.

Now it's Candy's turn to open her presents. She snatches Kevin's gift. "This is a big ol' box."

Kevin grins. "Hurry up and open it."

Inside the box is a huge teddy bear holding a heart in its hands. Um . . . I'm not sure if I authorize this gift!

"Thank you, Kevin. This is sweet! I'm gonna put him on my dresser so I can hug him every night before I go to sleep."

Ugh! Kevin is totally blushing. Are they crushing for real? Go figure!

We go back around and everyone else has their turns opening gifts. I get a purse from Hope and a pretty stationery set from Kevin.

Finally, it's time for Ricky to open my gift. He's saved mine for last, too. I feel like I'm sitting on pins and needles as he tears open the paper. He pulls away the tissue paper and gives a huge smile.

"Gia got me a Titans jersey! And a hat. This is fresh to death, Gia. Thank you!"

I'm so glad that he loves his gift! I get the feeling that if we weren't in a room full of our friends, he'd show me his appreciation with more than a smile. I guess that means it's a good thing that we're all down here together. Right?

Okay, I just gave myself the tight-lipped side eye.

Everyone's eyes are on me as I open the tiny box that has Ricky's name on it. I wouldn't be mad if it was another charm, because he picks the prettiest ones. But once I get the box open I see that it's not another charm. It's a beautiful, jeweled butterfly hair clip.

"It's gorgeous, Ricky," I gasp.

"There's a story behind it, and we're all fam here, so I'll tell it to everybody. It's supposed to be like symbolic of when a caterpillar turns into a butterfly."

I narrow my eyes. "You calling me a caterpillar?"

"No, but when we were in the ninth grade, you didn't have your style yet and you were still figuring out who Gia was," Ricky explains. "Now, you know who you are, and you're out of your cocoon, like a butterfly."

A single tear slides down my face. Yeah, a single tear. Don't hate. Please do not hate.

Hope gushes, "Aww . . . stop it!"

Kevin hurls a couch pillow at Ricky. "Yeah, man! You just broke man law with that gift. A butterfly?"

I wipe the tear away and crack up laughing with everyone else. My friends are the bomb diggity.

But back to Ricky and the random sentimental gift. I don't know what to say. He's been completely scary these past few weeks. First, he was on some "don't go acting all weird" stuff and now he's buying charms, planning birthday parties, and telling me I'm a butterfly. What gives?

I grab his arm, pull him into the pool-table room and close the glass door. Everyone can still see us, but they just can't hear our conversation.

"Ricky, what's up?" I ask.

"What's up with what?"

"Right before we went to state you asked me if I was gonna start acting weird over that charm bracelet. But you're the one acting . . . well you're not acting like yourself."

Ricky sighs and leans on the edge of the pool table. "I really like you, Gia."

"I know."

"You know? Wow, you're cocky, aren't you?"

"Not trying to be cocky, just trying to help you along."

Ricky laughs. "I like you, but I don't want us to stop being friends. So, I'm like really tripping on doing any of this stuff. But then I saw that bracelet, and I just had to get it because it made me think of you."

"And the barrette?"

"I thought it would look pretty in your hair," he replies. "Gia, you got me doing all kinds of sucka type stuff. That ought to count for something."

"It does count."

We're silent for a moment, but it's not awkward. It's like we're trying to regroup for round two. The lightning round.

"Can we not make it official just yet?" Ricky asks.

I bite my lip, not quite sure why we're waiting. "Sure, Ricky. I can wait."

He exhales a sigh—it sounds like relief. "Good. Because I wouldn't want you going off with some other dude, just because it wasn't official."

"Never that, Ricky Ricardo. Never that."

I don't know what to make of this conversation. Ricky just asked me if his gifts count for something. I guess they count toward him learning how to crush. But then he almost asked me to be his official girl.

Wow to infinity.

If my life was like a Disney sitcom, this would be the part where the magic of Christmas touches Gwen's cooking skills and she pulls off the perfect dinner. Um . . . yeah. Operative word—if.

My mom had refused any help in the kitchen from any of us, especially Aunt Penny. I think it mostly had to do with the fact that Aunt Penny bought her a cookbook for her Christmas gift.

Speaking of gifts, I got a whole bunch of clothes from my mom and LeRon, and gift cards from everyone else. Score! They know me so well.

On the table is a deeply browned turkey. Actually, it's nearly blackened. The pans of dressing and macaroni and cheese have a wet, soupy consistency and the yams look mushed and sticky. It's some of Gwen's best work!

Our whole family is seated around the table. Kevin and Ricky escaped soon after my mom declared she didn't want any help.

My uncle clears his throat. "Uh, let's bless the food."

"Somebody needs to read that turkey its last rites," Aunt Penny says with a giggle.

My mom glares at her sister all the way through the prayer.

After we say "amen," Grandma Stokes says, "Everything looks good, Gwendolyn. I'm proud of you."

I'm praying that a lightning bolt doesn't crack the sky and scorch my grandma for lying.

Pastor Stokes hands LeRon the carving knife. "Since your wife did the cooking, you can do the honors."

LeRon slices thin pieces of turkey and puts them on everyone's plates. From what I can tell, aside from the dark skin, the turkey seems to be fine. At least it looks done all the way through.

We all pass the side dishes and mostly everyone only takes enough for a bite or two. Everyone except LeRon, that is. He piles his plate high and stuffs his face like it's the best meal he's ever eaten. My mom's smile beams over in his direction, and she looks super happy.

I guess eating food that technically could be listed as a biohazard is the definition of love.

Sweet!

★ 25 ★

On the first day back from winter break, the hall-ways are buzzing with something. I don't know what, yet, because I just walked into the school. It must be high drama because Jewel and Kelani, wearing their matching Christmas outfits, are standing in front of my locker look-ing twisted.

"Hey, y'all," I say.

"Hey, Gia." Jewel's eyes go directly to my hair. "Ooh, that barrette is fly! Did you get that for Christmas?"

I nod. "Ricky gave it to me."

I know I didn't have to tell them that Ricky gave me the gift, but I'm ready to put our mutual crushes on public status. It's time for me to claim what's mine so that all the other potential crushees can sit down somewhere.

"You and Ricky are like that now? Okay!" Kelani pounds my fist and laughs.

"It's about time!" Jewel exclaims. "Y'all been playing games since ninth grade."

"So what's going on? What's everybody talking about?" I ask.

"Oh, you didn't hear?" Kelani says. "Valerie's mom got arrested over the weekend for cyber stalking. The police came right to their door on the day after Christmas and took her away."

My eyes feel like they're about to pop out of my head. Kelani explains, "Her neighbor's cousin called my mother's beautician and she gave my mom the scoop while she was getting her weave."

Whoa. Not the ten degrees of separation on the gossip tip.

"Are you serious?" I ask. "Is Valerie okay? Has anybody talked to her?"

"I haven't," Jewel says. "I tried to call her cell, but she hasn't been picking up."

"Did your mother's beautician have any details?" I ask.

"Only that whatever Valerie's mom was doing was the reason why Susan Chiang tried to kill herself. It had something to do with Facebook."

Jewel says, "The police had an anonymous tip, I think."

I am almost one hundred percent sure that Jewel can neither spell nor define "anonymous," but that's beside the point. The real issue here is that Valerie's mom got arrested. I thought she might get in trouble, but I didn't know they'd arrest her and put her in jail.

"That is messed up," I say.

"Here she comes now," Jewel says.

Valerie struts down the center hallway of Longfellow High and she looks like a teenage supermodel. Her hair is flat-ironed pin straight and parted down the center. She's got on a pink miniskirt (even though it's twenty-two degrees outside) and a shiny top that would look appropriate on most people only at a club.

And no, she does *not* have the audacity to be wearing pink-tinted sunglasses. I almost expect to see a little white dog pop his head up out of her purse.

"Hey, Hi-Steppers! Ooo-OOO!" Valerie says as she stops at my locker.

She seems to be in high spirits. Too high for someone whose mama got taken to the slammer.

"Hi, Valerie," I say. "How was your vacation?"

Valerie bursts into a flurry of laughter. "Cut the games, Gia. I know you and the twin bobble heads already know what happened with my mom. It's all over town."

I glance at Jewel and Kelani, who are trying to pretend like they're innocent. "Yes, we heard, of course. Are you okay?"

"I'm great! I just got finished talking to Mrs. Spencer, the senior counselor, and she said that all of those restrictions they had on me are lifted. I can go to the prom, I can graduate, and I can run for prom queen if I want to!"

"But aren't you upset about your mom?" I ask.

"Sure, but my uncle got her a good lawyer. He said that there's not really anything they can charge her with in our state. He said she'd be out on bail sometime this week."

"Is your mom going to apologize to Susan or anything?" I ask.

Valerie laughs again. "Um, probably not. My mom can't stand Susan or her parents."

Well, at least Valerie gets her evil honest. Her mom actually has her beat. I wonder how either one of them sleeps at night.

"Susan is back in school today," Kelani says. "You should probably stay away from her, Valerie."

"What for? I didn't do anything to her. She's the one who stole my Homecoming Queen title. My mother and I are not the same person."

I shake my head angrily. "Valerie, when are you going to let that go? Susan didn't steal anything from you. She won fair and square. You need to squash this, because it's way out of control."

"Shut up, Gia. You're always trying to rule somebody with your goody-goody self. Save it for your goody-goody lame church friends."

"My *lame* church friends? Why are you coming to our PGP meetings if you think we're lame?"

"I don't know. Tell your mom that I'm dropping out. A cotillion is a stupid idea anyway. I'm going to the prom in a few months."

I toss one hand up. "Whatever."

I slam my locker shut and walk away from Valerie, Jewel, and Kelani. Valerie calls after me. "Hey, Gia, do you want to put your detective hat on again? Someone snitched on my mother and I need to find out who it was."

"Nah, go find another goody-goody to help you out."

Valerie has sufficiently irritated me, so I appreciate seeing Ricky at the end of first period. He's standing at his locker, dressed in his Tennessee Titans jersey looking extra fine.

"Nice jersey," I say, sneaking up on him.

He smiles. "Thanks. A good friend bought it for me."

I lift my eyebrows. Good friend? I thought we'd moved beyond good friend into the almost-crush zone. Ricky stays flip-flopping. He's worse than the politicians my mom made me watch on CNN during the last election.

"Your good friend? Was it a guy friend, because if it was a girl, I'd say she might be more than a good friend," I reply.

"It is a girl, and she's my friend."

"Does that make her your *girlfriend*?"

Ricky laughs. "What's up, Gi-Gi? I see you're rocking your barrette."

"Yeah. Some dude gave it to me."

"Wow, okay. I'm *some dude* now?"

I shrug. "As long as I'm a good friend, you can be some dude."

Ricky takes his finger and trails a line down my arm and ends with my fingertips. His touch feels electric.

"You know you're more than a good friend, Gia."

Kevin, as usual, busts up our moment. "Hey, y'all! What it do?"

Kevin is wearing every single last one of his Christmas presents. New jeans, new boots, new suede jacket with furry collar, and new Cleveland Browns hat. The entire ensemble complements his tall, thin frame and the color scheme brings out the light brown flecks in his eyes. With a little bit more work, Kevin can be upgraded to full-time hottie.

"Hey, Kev," Ricky says. "Are we forcing Gia to learn to drive this week?"

Kevin nods. "Yep. It's past time, Gia. We need you to go ahead and do that. I'm not going to be driving you around New York City."

"I'll take the subway, Kevin. Everyone does."

Ricky interjects, "I know that you two are like the smartest kids in the class, but y'all do know that there is a chance that they might pick somebody else for this summer program."

Kevin laughs. "Not unless they're smoking something. And I'm planning to go to Columbia anyway, so I'm perfect. How could they not pick me?"

I have to agree with Kevin. If they pick anyone in our class it will be Kevin. Kev's had straight A's since he started kindergarten, and hasn't ever even had a detention. He's the poster child for anyone's enrichment program.

Kevin says, "Did y'all hear Valerie's mother got arrested? That's tripped out, huh?"

"For real?" Ricky asks. "Gia, why didn't you say something?"

"I was about to."

"You cool?" he asks.

Ricky is the only one who knows that I went to my uncle about this. I know he'll keep the secret, though, so I'm not even worried about that. Ricky is like a vault when it comes to secrets. They go in, but they don't come out. I love that about him.

"I'm good. And so is Valerie, by the way. She's planning to be the prom queen now."

Ricky laughs. "Dang, that girl stays trying to be the winner. Her mother might go to jail and she's planning for the prom."

"You can't say she's not prepared!"

Kevin points down the hall. "Here comes Hope."

She looks funny, racing at breakneck speed. What's even funnier is that I'm almost one hundred percent sure she's coming over here to tell us what we already know.

Hope leans on the locker, completely out of breath. "Did . . . y'all hear . . ."

"About Valerie's mom?" I ask. "Yes, we heard. The entire school has heard."

Hope shakes her head. "That's not what I was about to say. Valerie and Susan just got into a fight. Susan confronted Valerie and demanded an apology, and Valerie told her to kick rocks."

"What! Valerie just got *out* of trouble. Now she's starting fights? I thought she wanted to go to the prom."

"That's the thing! Valerie didn't start it. Susan swung on Valerie first. Smacked her so hard she flew into the lockers. Then Susan jumped on her and started scratching, pulling her hair, the works!"

Wow! Valerie got the smack-down from a lame. This is going to go down in Longfellow High history.

Kevin asks, "Did somebody break it up?"

"One of the counselors pulled Susan off of Valerie, and it was over. Valerie was screaming that she was pressing charges."

"I think someone needs to call Aunt Elena," I say. "Because fighting at school is against the PGP code of conduct."

Hope gasps. "You want to get Valerie kicked out of PGP?"

"She says we're a bunch of lames anyway. She should be happy we did!"

★ 26 ★

"In just three short months, we'll be having our PGP cotillion, announcing you as debutantes to all of your families and friends," Aunt Elena announces.

How about we all know the cotillion is coming? For most of the girls in the room, it's the only reason why they joined PGP in the first place. I'm looking forward to it, especially since Ricky is going to be my escort. It's going to be fiyah!

Speaking of the other girls, Valerie isn't here and we didn't even snitch on her about fighting. I heard my mom say that she'd quit the program. Oh well, guess she doesn't want to be powerful or pure!

But right now, I'm more concerned about taking that SAT test. The cotillion is probably last on my list of concerns right now.

About halfway through our meeting, the back door of the church opens and Sascha Cohen walks in. Aunt Elena stops her speech and looks to my mother for saving. She's gonna make my mom be the bad guy, I see.

"How can we help you, Ms. Cohen?"

Sascha clears her throat. "I just wanted to apologize to everyone in the program about the drama that I've brought to everyone. I also want to ask if I can rejoin the program. I am still pure and I haven't broken any rules."

My mother replies, "Okay, Sascha, since you are so determined to be a part of PGP, we'll allow you back in on a trial basis. If, between now and the cotillion, we observe any conduct that is unbecoming to a young lady in this program, we will ask you not to participate."

Sascha runs up to the front of the church and hugs Aunt Elena and then my mother. She looks so happy! I'm just glad my mother decided to stop acting like a dictator.

After we're dismissed, everyone goes up to Sascha to welcome her back. I wait until I'm the last one, because I've got some questions that I want to ask. No, this is not about being nosy, this is about looking out for my girl!

"Congratulations, Sascha," I say when it's finally my turn. "What made you come back?"

"I talked to my mom about it and she said that the worst they could do was say no."

Sascha's mom clearly does not know the carnage that my mom can cause. She could certainly do worse than saying no, but that's neither here nor there right now.

"Well, you're back in now. That's the most important thing. Chase isn't going to be your escort at the cotillion, is he?"

Sascha frowns. "Why wouldn't he be? He is my boyfriend, Gia. That hasn't changed."

"I just assumed you broke up with him and that's why you're coming back to us. My bad."

"I'm still with him, so yes, he'll be escorting me."

Somehow that sounds like a bad idea, but I'm not about to judge her. Even if I wanted to judge, I haven't got time. I've got to go over these SAT vocabulary flash cards one more time with Ricky and Kevin before we take our test tomorrow.

So Sascha and her manhandling boyfriend drama has to take a backseat.

"Pencils. Do you have pencils?" Kevin asks in the car on the way to the testing location.

"Kevin, I've got a whole box of pencils. I've never had more pencils for any test. I think I'm covered on pencils."

Kevin ignores my sarcasm. "What about you, Ricky? You good?"

"Yes, Kev. I've got pencils too."

Never before have I seen Kevin this fired up. He even drank coffee this morning. Well, it was a mocha caramel latte, but it was coffee nonetheless. He's wearing all black. A black turtleneck, black jeans, and black cardigan sweater.

"Kevin, what's with the all black?" I ask. "You look like you're about to rob a jewelry store."

"Opposite of funny. I'm in serious mode. These are serious clothes, because I've got my serious game face on."

The way he scrunches his eyebrows down so that they're nearly touching his nose does not look serious at all. Actually, it looks like utter hilarity, so Ricky and I burst into laughter. And not a couple of tee-hee giggles; I'm talking a lean-over laughter that makes your stomach muscles hurt.

"Silence!" Kevin screams.

This is even funnier, because Kevin is driving with one hand and the other is raised in a fist to the ceiling! Is he supposed to be scary?

"Stop it, Kevin," I beg. "You're gonna make me pee on myself."

"You had better not, Gia. I will pull off one of those afro puffs if you do."

Tears are rolling down my face now. Why does Kevin do this? The one time when I need to be focused and ready for business, and I'm laughing uncontrollably at Kevin's antics. Ricky's doubled over in the front seat too, so neither one of us can stop.

"Are you two ready to stop now?" Kevin asks. "We're at the testing location."

Ricky and I both breathe in and out, trying to stop the flow of laughter. As I relax, I realize that all of my tension about the test is gone. I think I needed that laugh to get my head in the game.

Now I'm cool, calm, and totally ready. I'm about to go in here and spank some SAT bootay! Holla!

★ 27 ★

It's been two and a half weeks since we took our SAT exam, and Kevin is about to have a meltdown. He's ready to get that score, and I don't blame him. I'm ready too.

The testing center gave us a password and told us that our scores would be available three weeks after we took the test. That leaves us just a few days. I'm trying not to be like Kevin and have my mind completely occupied with the test scores, so I'm doing something else.

Shopping for cotillion gowns with my mother, Aunt Elena, Hope, and Candy. Womp, womp on me.

"I want something strapless," Candy announces as we walk into a bridal store.

My mom replies, "Why don't you try something modest? This entire exercise is about purity and innocence, so I'm not letting you get some hoochie dress."

"And why does strapless have to mean hoochie? I've

seen several strapless gowns on the Oscars red carpet that scream class and sophistication! Nothing hoochie at all."

Everyone stops and gives Candy the blank stare. She should be used to receiving that look. She gets it almost daily from our crew.

I say, "I don't care what my dress looks like as long as it doesn't itch."

"I bet Ricky would like to see you in something flowery, since he called you a butterfly!"

My hand subconsciously goes to my butterfly barrette that I wear every day. "Shut up, Hope. What would Brother Bryan like to see you in?"

"Why does everyone keep making jokes about my escort?" Hope asks. "He's like a big brother to me. This is so not a date."

"As long as you know that," Aunt Elena says. "Your daddy would have a conniption fit if you tried to date someone as old as Brother Bryan."

First of all, no, I do not have an exact definition for conniption fit. It's one of those things that you know when you see it. Second, Brother Bryan is not that old. He's only twenty-five. Do they think we can't do math?

Plus, Brother Bryan is hotness personified.

Yep, just sprung an SAT word on you. You thought that after I took the test I'd be done using multisyllabic words? Womp on you. Deal with it.

"Candy, Kevin is escorting you, right?" my mom asks. "He's a good boy. Deacon and Mother Witherspoon are doing such a good job raising him."

"He's a cutie too!" Candy declares.

I riffle through a rack of white dresses and I don't see

one that I like. I don't want something formfitting, but that's what they mostly have on the racks.

"Gia! I've found the dress for you. It's perfect!" my mother squeals from the next rack over.

She's holding up a soft-white lace gown. It reminds me of something a Spanish princess would've worn during the 1800s. It's slightly off the shoulder and then it cinches in at the waist and flows out in a few layers of ruffles on the bottom. I've got to admit—it's breathtaking.

"Okay, Mom. Me likee."

For some reason, completely out of nowhere, my mom bursts into tears. I don't know how picking out a cotillion dress can trigger tears, but clearly it has.

"What's wrong, Mom?" I ask.

"I never got to do stuff like this when I was your age. I'm just so happy that you're a good girl, Gia. You just don't know."

"I'm happy too, Mom. I just want to make you proud."

My mother hugs me tightly, nearly crushing the dress. "You do make me proud, Gia. Every day."

Candy and Hope rush over and join in the hug. Every hug around those two turns into a group hug. They're just mushy like that.

"Is someone having a mother-daughter moment?" Aunt Elena asks.

"Yep, we sure are," my mom replies.

We *are* having a moment! And for the first time in a long list of moments, I don't mind at all!

The next day at school, I'm avoiding Kevin, so I take the long way to my first-period class. It's too early in the morning for me to deal with his hysteria. I can't wait for tomorrow so that he can log on to the test site and check his scores. It will be a lot easier for us all once he finds out.

I never go this way, and it's a nice change because the scenery is different. Even the lockers are a different color. They're red on this floor; on the first floor they're army green.

I turn down the hall leading to the tunnel that will take me across to my class, and guess who I see hugged up on the lockers. It's Chase and some girl who's absolutely not Sascha. He's so involved in his lip lock that I'm surprised the girl isn't choking on his tongue. Ewww!!

Chase has got to be the most disrespectful boy, ever. He's kissing on that girl all out in the open, not even caring if someone tells his girlfriend. That's foul.

I know that I shall not be the person to tell her. As a matter of fact, I'm gonna just act like I didn't see that. I've had more than my share of secrets this year, and I'm broken. I don't think that I could successfully carry another secret without spontaneously combusting.

"Chase!"

Looks like I won't have to keep a secret, because that was Sascha's voice screaming down the hall. Why aren't my feet moving? I can just go on to my class and not be concerned with this.

"Hey, Sascha. Have you met Tanya?"

My jaw drops open. No, he did not just introduce his kissing buddy to Sascha. I don't turn around, but I haven't taken any more steps toward my class.

"Chase, it's over," Sascha says. "I'm not dealing with this anymore."

A loud noise makes me turn around, and I see that Chase has Sascha pinned against the lockers. "It's over when I say it's over," he says.

"Let her GO!" I shout.

Chase looks back at me. "Gia, you better step if you know what's good for you."

"Or what? You're gonna put your hands on me? I wish you would."

Chase snarls. "Don't tempt me." He lets Sascha's hair go, and she stumbles away from the locker toward me. "You know what?" he asks. "I'm done too. You're just a little girl anyway."

Chase and Tanya walk down the hall in the opposite direction. Girls like Tanya get on my nerves. Why does she think that Chase won't do the same thing to her when he gets mad?

"You okay, Sascha?"

"Yeah, I'm done with that loser."

"You might be done, but he sure left you with a gift to remember him by," I say while peering at her rapidly swelling eye.

"I feel my eye puffing up."

Not only is that eye puffed, it's going to be black too. I know my mom is going to ask her about it at the next PGP meeting.

"Do you think you should go to the nurse's office?"

Sascha shakes her head. "Then they'll ask me how it happened, and they'll make me file a police report on

Chase. I've tried to report this before, but I didn't want Chase getting in any real trouble."

"You're kidding me, right? He's not your boyfriend anymore, so now we don't care how much trouble he's in."

"You don't understand, Gia. He doesn't mean to be like this. His dad hits him all the time."

"That doesn't mean he gets to use you as a punching bag."

Sascha replies, "Just go to class and let me handle this, Gia."

"You *are* breaking up with him, right?"

She nods sadly. "Yes, Gia. I'm breaking up with him."

"Okay. Well, let me walk you to wherever you're going in case he comes back."

"But you'll be late for class."

"I've got a sneaking suspicion that my teacher will understand."

After school, I come straight home. The past few months have been exhausting, and I think I just need to rest. No crew, no Ricky, no nothing. Just chillaxin' in my bed with my boy Tweety.

Unfortunately, my mom has other plans.

"Gia, did you know that Sascha's boyfriend gave her a black eye at school today?"

I nod. "Ex-boyfriend. She was breaking up with him, that's why she got a black eye."

"So you were there while they fought?" she asks.

"They weren't exactly fighting. It happened so fast. One second he was kissing another girl, and then the next second, he was slamming Sascha into the lockers. I couldn't have done anything even if I wanted to."

"She's out of the program. I just got finished talking to her mother. I should've gone with my first mind on this."

"But why is she out again? Because she got a black eye?"

"No, because she stayed with that abusive boy."

"But he gave her the black eye when she broke up with him. Mom, you're not being fair. You're punishing Sascha for things that Chase has done and he doesn't have any consequences at all."

My mother replies, "Who says he doesn't have any consequences? I'm reporting his cowardly behind to the authorities."

"But you're kicking Sascha out. Again."

"Yes. I should've never let her back in the first time."

I shake my head to show my disagreement. "It's not fair, and I don't agree."

Gwen smiles. "Oh well, too bad you don't have to agree!"

I wonder how she'd feel if we *all* disagreed?

★ 28 ★

I type in my password on the SAT test results site. I haven't told my mother that I can check them today, because I didn't want her to hound me about getting my score. I've already got Kevin hounding me and that's bad enough.

He and Ricky checked their scores earlier and they both did well. Kevin scored a 1512 and Ricky got a 1435. My friends are totally smart!

I don't know why it's taken me all day to check mine, but right now is the moment of truth. I take the mouse and click the Log In button, and close my eyes.

Just when I'm about to open them wide, Candy screams over my shoulder, "You got a 1548!"

"W-what? I did?" I ask.

Then I look at the screen and see the numbers right there in my face for me to look at. I got a 1548. Higher than

Kevin and probably anyone else in my school. This is beyond awesome.

"That's so good, Gia. You'll probably be able to go to any school you want!" Candy gushes.

"I want to go to Spelman, I think."

"Ooh, that will be hot, and I can come visit you on campus and go to frat parties. I cannot wait. Will you please hurry up and graduate!"

"I've got a year and a half left, Candy, so you can wipe the drool off your face."

My mom comes into the living room from her bedroom. "What is all the noise about?"

"Gia got a 1548 on her SAT!"

Can I share my own news? Dang!

"Congratulations! Have you called Ricky and Kevin yet?"

"No, and Hope doesn't take hers until the spring."

"I'm sure she'll do well too."

I'm sure my mother can feel the arctic breeze that I'm sending her way. If it wasn't for the test results, we wouldn't even be having a conversation right now. I'm still salty about her kicking Sascha out the program for a second time, but I have launched a counterattack.

Every girl in PGP says that they think Sascha should be a part of our cotillion. She's earned it and I think she should be rewarded for not giving that jerk her virginity.

We've all decided that we will be presented together or not at all. My mom and Aunt Elena will trip if all the girls decide to boycott the cotillion. Especially my aunt, because she's invited half of the pastors and their wives from all over the city.

Sounds like a good plan, right?

Anyway, with my SAT score nailed on the first try, I can relax somewhat when it comes to picking my school. Spelman is my number one choice, but I'm open to other places as long as they have a dance squad and give me scholarship money. My mom likes Spelman because it's all girls. Right. She would.

My phone buzzes on the desk. The text says I know you told, Gia. Thanks. Valerie.

I don't respond, because I don't think a response is required. I'm not going to confirm or deny her suspicions that it was me who opened my mouth, but I am glad she appreciates me for being the goody-goody that I am.

Candy looks out the living room window. "Ricky and Kevin are here."

My mom looks at me suspiciously. "Are you all going out?"

"Not that I know of," I answer—which is readily apparent by the raggedy sweats and slippers that I'm wearing.

Candy opens the door and they storm in. "Hey, Sister Gwen. We're kidnapping Gia today."

It's Saturday morning, so a kidnapping is not out of the question. But what, pray tell, are they kidnapping me for? I'm not in the mood for any foolishness or shenanigans. Hahaha. Just had to laugh at my random use of shenanigans. I've been hanging around Kevin and his tomfoolery for too long.

Kevin says, "We're forcing her to learn how to drive, Sister Gwen. She's beyond ready."

My mom laughs. "I happen to agree. She's all yours. I

need someone to start running my errands, going to the grocery store, and dropping Candy off at rehearsals."

What?!?! Gwen wants me to be her personal slave and that's why she's on board with my driving lessons! I'm totally slayed by this revelation.

Candy hands me a pair of tennis shoes. "Get out!"

"Can I at least comb my hair and brush my teeth? Or do you all want to be treated to dragon-breath Gia?"

"Please do," Ricky replies. "And do something about those funky looking sweats too."

"Shut all the way up, boy!" I throw a jab at Ricky's gut. "By the way, in case anyone was wondering, I got a 1548 on my SAT."

"What a geek!" Kevin says. Coming from him, I know it's all in love.

"I can't believe you scored higher than Kevin," Ricky says.

Kevin smiles. "I was stressed about that thing. I'm glad it's over."

I take about twenty minutes to get presentable—not exactly fly—because that takes more than twenty minutes. I'm rocking jeans and my powder blue Tweety sweatshirt. If I'm going to learn to drive today, Tweety most definitely needs to be in the mix.

"Let's do this," I say.

Today is another good day for driving. It's February, so it's not like it's warm, but there's no snow anywhere to be seen.

Ricky starts the car and says, "To the park, right?"

"What? You think I'm driving down the street? Boy, quit playing."

Kevin laughs out loud. "We thought you were gonna nail this today, Gia. You've been pretending to learn for months."

"Whatever, dude."

Ricky says, "I have an announcement to make."

"What?" I ask.

"I'm calling a cease and desist on Valentine's Day. It's too much pressure. I *just* had to find a birthday gift and a Christmas gift for you, Gia. Please, can I get away with a card?"

Kevin and I stare at him. What kind of foolishness is this? You can't just call a moratorium on a holiday. Especially a holiday that is tailor-made for crushes. Who does he think he is?

"I don't think that's allowed," Kevin finally says. "Am I right, Gia?"

"Ricky doesn't have to do anything he doesn't want to do. If he has a valentine, then he should most probably get her a gift. That would be the right thing to do."

Ricky chuckles quietly. I don't know why he would think that I would let him off the hook for Valentine's Day. Out of all the years that I've been valentine-less, there's no way I'm going to have a crush and still look like a lonely girl on that day.

Kev asks, "So are y'all together now? Because nobody is sure about that."

I clear my throat and wait for Ricky to answer. He says, "Gia and I are in like mode right now, Kev. Not *together,* but I don't want her talking to anyone else, so if you've got any plans for her . . ."

"Yeah, right," Kevin replies with a chuckle. "The crew is just nosy."

"Wait a minute!" I say. "How are you trying to keep me from talking to anybody else, but you're not trying to make me your official girl?"

Ricky looks surprised. "Do you want to talk to somebody else?"

"No, but if I did, I wouldn't feel bad, because I don't have a boyfriend. I have a *good friend* who buys me stuff."

Real talk. Ricky's fear of being called the "boyfriend" is excessive and unnecessary. We've already established that our world won't change if we take that step, and it's not like I'm gonna pressure him to do anything he doesn't want to do.

As a matter of fact, it's got me pretty heated right now. When Ricky stops the car and parks, I get behind the wheel. Maybe it's the adrenaline from being mad, but I'm not afraid at all.

"You ready?" Ricky asks.

I narrow my eyes, click the seat belt closed, and slam the car into drive.

"Hold up! Easy on the ride!" Ricky says.

I peel out across the parking lot and do a sharp turn at the end like I've been driving my whole life. Then I slow down, put the car in reverse, and back into one of the parking spots. I've always been afraid to go in reverse, but not today.

"Very good, Gia!" Kevin exclaims.

"I think I'm ready to drive on the road," I say.

"You do have your temporary permit, so go ahead," Ricky says.

Can someone explain to me why he's grinning so hard? I don't see anything funny, cute, or grin-worthy. I want to wipe that silly smile right off his face.

I pull out of the parking lot and drive down the winding road that leads away from the park. I feel my heartbeat start to race a little bit when I see the oncoming traffic. That's always been the biggest thing for me. Those other cars. What if they don't stop when they're supposed to?

"Put on your right turn signal and get ready to turn," Ricky instructs.

"I know."

Ricky laughs like he's unconcerned with my attitude. "Well, do it then."

I flick on the turn signal and look out at the two-lane street. The traffic is very light because who comes to the park in Ohio in February?

I take a deep breath and then ease onto the street. I take us up to the speed limit and cruise there. In the immediate distance, I see a red light.

"Okay, Gia. You see the red light up ahead, so just ease on the brake and start to slow down."

I follow Ricky's instructions now, because I've never gone this far before! I'm driving! I'm at a red light and I'm on the street with other cars! *Sweet!*

"Take us back to your house," Ricky says.

"You sure?"

"Yeah. You got this."

I totally do have this. And even though I'm still mad at Ricky for his indecisiveness, I'm glad he pulled that out of the box today. Because I'm driving now! Look out, pedestrians!

★ 29 ★

"**W**hat did you get Ricky for Valentine's Day?" Hope whispers in our super boring government class.

"The same thing he got me. Nothing. He wants to skip Valentine's Day this year."

"Hmmm . . . that's not what I heard."

"What do you mean, that's not what you heard?"

"You know I'm on the sweethearts committee this year, and we're delivering carnations all day today."

"Ricky got me a carnation?"

"Well, I can't say for certain, but if I was you, I'd get him one too. They're still selling them in the hallway."

Hope wouldn't say this if it wasn't the absolute truth. She plays games sometimes, but not on something like this.

"When are the flowers being delivered?" I ask.

"Starting fifth period. They're a dollar apiece."

I raise my hand and ask for a bathroom pass. It's not an untruth! I will go to the bathroom while I'm out there.

I walk up to the rally girls' "Sweethearts" table with my dollar out. One dollar seems like an awfully cheap valentine, so I pull out another one. I'll get him two.

"Who is this for?" rally girl Chloe asks. "Ricky Free-man, right?"

I nod. "Do I get to put a note with it?"

"Yep. What do you want to say?" Chloe asks as she takes out her glitter-pink marker to write.

May I object to the pen being glittery and pink? I would prefer blue ballpoint for the note I'm sending.

"Umm . . . I guess just put, 'from your good friend, Gia.'"

Chloe scrunches up her nose. "That's all?"

I nod. "Yep. That's it."

"Okay."

Chloe whips out that pen like she's some kind of Pi-casso and writes the note in big curly letters. And then she has the audacity to put a heart over the I in my name. A simple dot would've been more than sufficient.

Chloe then hands the note to another rally girl and says, "Here. We've got another one for Ricky Freeman."

Another one? Another one! Wow. I see why he's trying to avoid Valentine's Day.

By the time I make it back into the classroom, I'm seething and Hope can tell. "What's wrong with you?" she whispers.

"Mr. Playa has a whole stack of flowers getting deliv-ered to him."

"So what? Ricky's been having girls chase him for like *ever!*"

"It's just that he wanted to cancel Valentine's Day this year. He said he didn't want to exchange gifts. I'm thinking he's tapped out buying for all his other crushes."

Hope rolls her eyes. "Girl, bye! He's tapped out spending all of his money on you. He went broke throwing your birthday party and he bought that little butterfly at the jewelry store."

"Well . . ."

"Are you a gold digger, Gia?"

"What?"

"I'm just saying. Here's something else for you to think about. Ricky might be getting a lot of carnations, but how many did he send?"

I shrug. "I don't know."

"Well, I do. And there's only one girl getting anything from Ricky today."

I sit back in my chair and smile. "For real?"

"Yeah. Gia, you're so spoiled, it's ridiculous."

"I am not."

"You are, but it's cool. As long as Ricky likes it."

"Did Kevin send any flowers?"

Hope nods. "He got some too, and not just from Candy."

"Get out! Candy sent him a carnation?"

"Yep! If you weren't so busy being wrapped up in your own dysfunctional crush, you'd see that they really dig each other."

I'm not that wrapped up in Ricky. I've known for a long time about Candy liking Kevin and vice versa. I was the first person to know, in fact.

"You know who else got a bunch of carnations?" Hope whispers.

"Who?"

"Sascha. She got a whole dozen of them from Chase."

"Eww! He's gross."

I can't believe he's trying to get back with Sascha after what happened in the hallway. I wonder if she's going to take him back. Honestly, I wouldn't put it past her, but I hope she's feeling powerful right about now!

Two hours later, it's sixth-period Trig and I'm stoked about getting my Valentine's Day flowers from Ricky. I'm just glad that he and Kevin aren't in this class with me.

I tap my pencil on the desk until the inevitable rally girl sticks her head in our door.

"Mr. Roscoe," rally girl Chloe sings, "I've got a special delivery."

Every girl in the class perks up, even the ones who got a delivery last period, because Chloe has a huge bunch of carnations in her hand.

Mr. Roscoe rolls his eyes and lets Chloe into the classroom. Guess he's not romantic. He's probably getting his wife a protractor for Valentine's Day. Boo, Mr. Roscoe.

Chloe walks up to my desk wearing a huge smile on her face. "Happy Valentine's Day, Gia."

Then, she hands me the entire bundle of carnations. There's got to be at least fifteen here.

"Are these all for me?" I ask.

"Yep. Somebody's sure crushing hard on you."

Wow. Now, I feel completely bad for only buying two! So much for the moratorium.

I take out the card and read the note. It says, "Hope these make you smile. Your BFF, Ricky."

I'm so not one of those girls who cries when I'm happy,

but I feel a tear in the corner of my eye. I wipe it away quickly before anyone sees.

"If all of the romance is done," Mr. Roscoe says, "then we can get back to work."

Ha! Maybe he can get back to work, but I'm not going to be able to concentrate on anything for the rest of the day!

Kevin and Ricky are already sitting at our lunch table when Hope and I arrive. It's pizza day in honor of the holiday, so I'm about to score some. I drop my bag and start toward the line.

"I got your lunch, Gia!" Ricky says. "Happy V day."

He pushes a tray into my spot. Yummy. There's a little card on there too. Awww . . . a valentine.

I open it and it's a little kid's card. Dora the Explorer is on there saying *"Vamanos!* Have a Happy Valentine's Day."

"You are so corny, Ricky."

"You're smiling."

Kevin asks, "Hope, who's your valentine this year? You've been super quiet on the crush scene."

"No crush for me. I'm just chillaxin' this year."

The tiny smile on Hope's face tells me she's hiding something. She's keeping a secret and methinks it's a secret crush.

She better be glad that Inspector Gia is burned out right now or I'd be all up and through her business. Because that's what I do!

★ 30 ★

Operation Cotillion is in full effect. We've got Sascha's dress (borrowed from a bridal shop), shoes (snuck from Aunt Elena's closet), and accessories (donated from the rally girls). She's still broken up about her breakup with Chase, so we've decided against a formal escort. We also decided that it was best for Sascha to try on her dress over at Hope's house. Gwen's mess radar is still in full effect and Aunt Elena is at church, so it should be cool.

"I'll look stupid," Sascha says as she tries on her dress in front of Hope's mirror. "Everyone else is going to have an escort. I'll just stick out like a sore thumb. Maybe I just won't go at all."

"You're going!" Candy says. "After everything we've done to help you, you're going."

I have a total brainstorm. "What if we all walk in together? Kevin, Ricky, and Brother Bryan can walk in behind us, but we can all walk in, arm in arm."

Hope's eyes widen. "Your mom is going to be mad."

"She's going to be mad regardless. But I don't agree with her, so whatever."

I'm over my mother's ridiculous decision to keep Sascha out of the cotillion. She broke up with Chase and begged for forgiveness. There's no way they should've kept her out.

"PGP belongs to us, right?" I ask.

Candy nods. "Yeah. It's powerful girls and not powerful grown ladies!"

"Since this is our cotillion, I think we should say who stays and who goes. I'm happy that Sascha kicked Chase to the curb, so I say she stays!"

Sascha asks, "Aren't you afraid you'll get grounded?"

To be honest, the thought had occurred to me. Especially, since I'm waiting on the acceptance letter to the summer enrichment program. It would not be fresh if I couldn't go to New York City. Not fresh at all.

But this is more important. This is about doing the right thing. And whether my mom realizes it or not, this is totally the right thing to do.

Hope asks, "Sascha, are you happy you broke up with Chase?"

"Sometimes. But I miss him, you know? I really thought he was going to be my first."

"It's good that he wasn't, because he is a dog!" Candy says.

"Not all the time. Do y'all know he bought me a dozen carnations a month ago on Valentine's Day?"

"We know, and we're not impressed," I say. "Those little raggedy carnations are not something to get excited about!"

Hope laughs out loud. "This coming from the girl who carried five dead carnations in her bag for a week."

Those were from Ricky. No explanation needed. Next!

"I just keep thinking about how sweet he can be when he wants to," Sascha says. "But I know it's just an act because he always goes back to being mean."

In the back of my mind, I wonder if Sascha would've broken up with Chase if she hadn't caught him kissing another girl in the hallway. Maybe she would've kept letting him hit her as long as his kisses were only for her.

"It's okay," Hope replies. "You'll find another guy that really deserves you."

"And maybe he'll marry you!" Candy adds.

Marriage? Wow, I can't even believe we're having this conversation. Getting married seems like it should be light-years away—no—millions of light-years away. We're still in high school, for heaven's sake.

"Y'all tripping, talking about getting married. We've still got college!"

"Isn't that where you're supposed to find your husband?" Hope asks.

"In the name of everything that is good and pure!" I exclaim. "Hope, please tell me you're not planning on going to college to find a husband."

"Of course, I'll get a degree while I'm there too, but my mom told me to find my husband in college. She knows what she's talking about. That's where she met my dad."

So, Aunt Elena and Uncle Robert met while they were in college. Aunt Elena ended up never finishing because they got married their sophomore year and she had Hope the same year. Aunt Elena's always talking about how she should've gotten her degree, and it sounds like Hope is planning to follow in her mother's footsteps. Wow.

Candy walks across the room and puts her iPod into Hope's iStereo. "Enough talk about getting married and college! Ugh! I need some music up in here."

Rihanna's "Take a Bow" flows from the speakers. Of course we all sing along, because we know the words.

Sascha sings along too, but there's a look of sadness in her eyes. Maybe we shouldn't be listening to a song about a breakup. But, for real, it's more than appropriate.

"Gia, I got the letter!" Kevin is screaming so loud into the phone that I can barely understand him.

"What are you talking about, Kev? What letter?"

He slows down and takes a deep breath. "From the summer enrichment program. I got in! I got in!"

"Oh, sweet! Now at least I know if I get in, I won't be up there by myself."

"Did you check the mail? The letter came today."

"I don't think our mail has been delivered."

"I hope you get to go, Gia. This will be fresh to infinity! Can you imagine the fun we'd have in New York City? We'll go to Broadway shows, we'll see the Statue of Liberty, we'll go jogging in Central Park!"

Excited much?

"Kev, I'll call you back when I find out, okay?"

"Okay."

Here's the thing: I don't know if I really want to be in the program now. They're only accepting two people from each grade in each participating school. So that means that if Kevin got in, and I get in, then I'll be spending the entire summer without Ricky. That would be a total bummer, especially since we've been getting closer over the past few months.

What if I'm gone for the summer and his crush fades? Or worse, what if he meets some hot girl over the summer and starts crushing on her? That would be all bad.

So as much as I want to be in the summer program, I'm hoping that I don't get that letter.

Dang, I sound almost as bad as Hope talking about finding a husband while she's in college. I would be totally dogging her out if she was even considering not taking an opportunity like this one because of a boy. That is such an un-Gia-like thing to do.

My cell phone buzzes on my hip. It's a text from Ricky. Didn't make it into the summer program. Did u?

Oh, no. Now it's totally possible that I'm going to get a letter telling me that I'm going to New York. The worst part is going to be breaking it to Kevin that I'm not going. But, real talk, what would be even worse than that would be coming back home and Ricky kicking it with someone else.

My mom walks through the door with an armful of bags. "Gia, will you give me a hand?"

I take two of the bags from her and set them on the table. Immediately, I start peeking in to see if she bought anything good. In the bags I have, I see only generic-brand cereal. Someone needs to explain to Gwen that Fruity-O's do not taste like the real thing. Not at all.

"You got a letter, Gia," my mom says.

Of course. I take the letter from my mother and turn it

over in my hands. It's from Columbia University, so I know it's the acceptance letter into the program.

"Aren't you going to open it?" she asks. "I see it's from the college. Is it about that summer program you all signed up for?"

I slowly rip open the envelope and take the letter out. I bite my lip anxiously when I read the very first word— *Congratulations.*

"You didn't get in? Maybe next time, honey," my mom says in her consoling tone. "Do you want to go up to the mall later to get job applications?"

"No, I did get in."

"Then why are you looking so sad?"

Okay, it's completely and totally impossible for me to share this with my mom without all of her parental unit radars going off. I don't want her to trip, nor do I want a mother-daughter bonding chat.

"No reason! I'm cool. Can you take me to get some new outfits to rock over the summer?"

"Sure. Kevin's going too, right?"

"Yep. He's already got our travel itinerary all mapped out."

"Perfect! I knew he would."

"Who says I'm gonna hang with him for the whole summer? I might meet some hotties up there with some Jay-Z swagger."

Gwen frowns. "You better make sure you're going up there for educational purposes, not boys. I'm going to have Kevin give me a weekly report."

"Ma, you're playing, right? You can trust me."

"I know, Gia. If I didn't trust you, I wouldn't be letting you go."

It's irritating to me how pumped my mom is about the summer program. She would not be this cool if Ricky was the one going. This summer is soooo *not* going to rock.

★31★

"You two look beautiful!" LeRon gushes as Candy and I stand in the living room in our cotillion gowns.

"Thank you, Daddy!"

"Thanks, LeRon."

My mom has tears in her eyes. She's had them in there since we started getting ready this afternoon.

"Mama Gwen, why are you crying?"

"Because you all are just growing up so quickly and I can't do anything to stop it."

"Duh! You're not supposed to stop it!" I reply with a laugh.

My cell phone rings in my purse. "Talk to me."

"Gia, I have a code red emergency going on right now and I need your help!"

It's Kevin and he really does sound like he's having an emergency. He sounds scared and sick at the same time.

"What's wrong, Kev?"

"M-my grandparents aren't letting me go to New York."

"What? Why not?"

"They said that they don't feel safe with me going to a city that's a target for terrorist attacks."

"Wow. I'm sorry, Kevin. Are you okay? Is there anything I can do?"

"No, I'm not good, but there's nothing you can do to help. I just wanted to tell you that our fun summer is cancelled."

"Aw, Kev. That's not cool. Try to chill, okay? At least until after the cotillion. We'll talk about it then."

When I press End on the phone, everyone is looking at me. "What's wrong with Kevin?" Candy asks.

"Deacon and Mother Witherspoon are not letting him go to the summer program. They said it's too dangerous."

"Oh, I'm sorry to hear that," my mom says. "I know he was looking forward to it."

"What does that mean for Gia?" LeRon asks.

Um, hello! Since when did the Witherspoon household have anything to do with Gia?

"Is anyone else from Longfellow High going to go?" my mom asks.

"I think they go down the list and pick the third person. But I don't know who else applied," I answer.

"Let's discuss this later, after the cotillion."

Umm . . . yeah. Nothing to discuss.

The youth ministry has transformed the recreation room at our church into a ballroom. It looks fancy, just like a wedding reception.

All of the PGP girls are standing in the back of the recreation hall in our white dresses. Soon we'll have to line up with our escorts and walk in to be presented before our family and friends.

I whisper to Hope, "Have you seen Sascha?"

"No. She's not here yet. She sent me a text saying that her parents were running late."

"She better hurry up before this whole rebellion was for nothing."

Just then, Sascha and her mom rush in through the rear door.

"Are we too late?" Sascha asks.

"No, girl. Come on and get in line."

Aunt Elena and my mom come out into the foyer, and Sascha's mom goes into the room with all the other parents. They both look excited, and so far neither of them has noticed that Sascha is here. Wouldn't it be great if they didn't notice until the ceremony starts?

"Excuse me, Sascha. Why are you here?" my mother asks.

So much for wishful thinking.

"Mom, we all decided that it was unfair for Sascha to be left out of the cotillion," I say.

"You *what?*"

My mother is taking very short breaths through her nose, and it almost makes her look like a bull that's getting ready to charge.

"We, the members of PGP, accept Sascha and applaud her for making the decision to walk away from a tough situation," Hope says, repeating the speech that I wrote for her.

"And as a collective, we have decided that if Sascha is not allowed to participate, that none of us will participate," Candy says.

My mother looks about ready to explode, but Aunt Elena seems very calm. She says, "I appreciate the fact that you all have come together as a unit to solve a problem. One of the goals of PGP is for you all to discover your inner leader. That said, it would've been more appropriate for you all to approach us prior to the cotillion."

"You wouldn't have listened to us if we'd done that," I reply.

She knows that it's true too. The only thing we have going for us right now is the element of surprise. Also, the embarrassment factor for the grown folk.

My mom sighs. Hopefully that is a sign of defeat!

"I, too, agree that you all have learned a valuable lesson about leadership and about dating violence," my mom says. "I do not think that Sascha should participate, but I do want the rest of you to enjoy this special moment. So, we will allow Sascha to be presented."

Everyone cheers in the foyer like we're at a football game. Sascha is close to tears.

"Calm down, ladies," Aunt Elena fusses. "You're supposed to be debutantes, not rowdy sports fans!"

My mom opens the door and allows the boys to come in to line up. Yes, Ricky is looking really good. I catch a few girls giving him double-take side eye. It's all good, though, because he's not looking back.

Sascha whispers to me, "I thought we were all walking in together. I don't have an escort."

"Yes, you do! You can share mine," I say. "Ricky, come here. Stand between us."

Ricky smiles. "Okay. Wow, I get two pretty girls."

"Watch yourself," I say.

"Shh!" Candy hushes. "We're starting!"

Next we hear my mother's voice on the microphone. "These girls have worked really hard to exemplify qualities that will bring honor to God. Above all, these gems are pure and ready to be presented to the world. We give you the PGP debutantes!"

There is a loud round of applause as the doors open! Aunt Elena reads off each of our names, ending with Sascha. Everyone stands and claps again as we circle the room on the arms of our escorts.

They look so proud of us! And I'm most definitely proud too. I'm happy that I can hold my head up high and shout out that I'm pure. That's just a ridiculous amount of hotness right there.

Sascha and I are each holding one of Ricky's arms as we circle the room, but he's only looking at me.

After we're finished walking, all of the debutantes sit at a long table with our escorts. We've got people waiting on us hand and foot, serving our dinner. It's kind of like we're a huge bridal party, but nobody got married.

My mom leans behind me and whispers in my ear. "Congratulations, Gia. I'm proud of you."

I look up into her face to see if there's any hint of retribution or an impending punishment for our rebellion. But she's nothing but smiles and joy. Whew! Why do I feel like I came super close to losing my life today?

After the dinner is over, we get to have a dance with our escorts. I let Sascha have Ricky and I dance with my uncle. Hope looks like she's in heaven dancing with grown Brother Bryan. I think Aunt Elena needs to check that immediately, but I'm not getting in that one! I've had enough drama.

Pastor Stokes says, "Thanks for the dance, Gia. I was sure you'd want to dance with Ricky."

"Oh, it's just Ricky."

He raises an eyebrow. "Just Ricky? I was led to believe that it was a little bit more than *just* Ricky."

"I don't know who you're getting your information from. You need a new source."

Pastor holds his head back and laughs. "One day I'll be dancing with you at your wedding."

"That's a long way off! I've got college!"

"College. It seems like I was just burping you on my shoulder. You know your mom and aunt used to leave me with you and Hope when you were babies."

"Really?"

"What? I was pretty good at it."

I laugh out loud. "Umm . . . I'm talking about my mom and Aunt Elena hanging out."

"Don't let them fool you! They were almost best friends until I became a pastor."

"Wow. I learn something new everyday."

Ricky walks up and taps Pastor Stokes on the shoulder. "Can I steal your partner, Pastor Stokes?"

"Well, Gia. It's *just* Ricky. Am I being kicked to the curb?"

I'm smiling hard. "Sorry, Pastor."

Ricky takes my hand. "Guess what?"

"What?"

"I'm going to New York!"

"What? How do you know?"

"Because my letter said that I was the third candidate and that they would contact me if there was a cancellation."

I feel my hands tremble. "I can't believe this! Oh my goodness, this is gonna be so fun."

"I know, right."

"But my mom is gonna trip if she thinks we're dating. She might not let me go."

Ricky nods. "Maybe we should chill on the crush thing for now. That way we can make sure there's no blocking."

As much as I hate to agree, I know this is the truth. If Ricky and I start skipping through the dandelions holding hands, my mom will put the halt on the summer program. And faking it won't work either, because my mom is nearly impossible to fool.

"Cool."

Ricky grins wickedly and says, "So does that mean I can holla at the fine ladies I'm going to meet at Columbia University?"

"What are you asking me for? I'm your friend, right? But if you can't find me around campus, I'm probably at Coney Island with my new boo."

"Jokes, I see."

"Are they jokes? Really?" I ask. "If you don't claim me, then I'm free, right."

Ricky pulls me in a little closer, but still far enough away to not raise any red flags to my mom. "I might not be claiming you out loud, but you know what it is, Gia."

He looks so serious when he says this, that my heart skips a little. But still, Ricky always comes short of really laying it all on the line, even when it's just between us. Now, like every other time, he almost makes me his official boo.

And everybody knows . . . Almost doesn't count.

IT'S ALL GOOD

Nikki Carter

ABOUT THIS GUIDE

The following questions are intended to
enhance your group's reading of
IT'S ALL GOOD.

Discussion Questions

1. What do you think about PGP (Powerful Girls are Pure)? Was it a lame idea? Why or why not?

2. Do you want to see Gia and Ricky together as a couple? Will it ruin their friendship?

3. Have you ever been cyber stalked? Has anyone ever posted a lie about you on the Internet? What was that like?

4. Were you surprised to find out who Susan's cyber stalker was? What would you do if you were being stalked?

5. Have you ever been in a relationship with someone who abused you? If you had a friend in this kind of relationship, would you tell someone?

6. Do you think it was fair for Valerie and Sascha to ask Gia to keep their secrets? Was Gia a snitch for telling?

7. Should Ricky and Gia claim each other over the summer, or should they put their crush on hold?

Sixteen Random Things About Gia

Okay, here are sixteen things about me from my Face-book page. After you read them, go on Nikki Carter's Facebook page—http://profile.to/nikkicarter—and post six-teen random things about you!

1. I sleep on my left side.

2. If my left side hurts, then I've got issues.

3. I'm allergic to snow and all temperatures below forty degrees.

4. I don't like bugs. They are not cute. Mostly, they're gross. Especially ones with lots of legs.

5. My favorite food is spaghetti. No, not my mom's spaghetti—hers is always crispy. Spaghetti should not crunch.

6. I make up random rules, like the one above. If spa-ghetti crunches, it should be issued a citation.

7. Swimming is my favorite sport.

8. Combing my afro puffs after swimming is my least favorite sport.

9. I'm a really good friend.

10. My mom is my role model.

11. I like classical music, like the kind they make you listen to in music class. Yeah, it rocks.

12. I think *Star Trek* is hotter than *Star Wars*.

13. I write lots of stuff in my journal that the world will never know about.

14. I think I'm exceptionally cute. So should you!

15. I'd like to have children one day . . . far, far in the future.

16. Save the Hi-Stepper! Save the world! Hahahaha!

A Discussion with the Author

1. **Coke or Pepsi?**
   Pepsi.

2. **What are your favorite TV shows?**
   Friday Night Lights, Smallville, Grey's Anatomy,
   and *Heroes.* (Save the cheerleader, save the world!!!
   Yeah!)

3. **Bath or shower?**
   Both.

4. **What's your most embarrassing moment?**
   I was at a house party in my good friend's basement. I went upstairs to get a snack and when I
   headed back downstairs, I slipped and fell down
   the flight of stairs. The music stopped, but I just
   hopped up and started dancing. Trust . . . it was
   ALL bad!

5. **Who's your favorite actress?**
   Sanaa Lathan! *Love and Basketball* is one of my
   favorite movies!

6. **Who's your favorite actor?**
   I have more than one. Johnny Depp, Denzel Wash-
   ington, and Idris Elba!

7. Who's your favorite singer?

   This changes a lot. Right now, I'm feeling Beyoncé, Alicia Keys, and Jennifer Hudson. I also like fun gospel artists like KiKi Sheard.

`8. Have you ever been in love?

   Yes!

9. If you could be a celeb for a day, who would you be?

   Hmm . . . Kimora Lee! She is running thangs. So fabulous!

10. Flip-flops or Crocs?

    Umm . . . neither.

11. What should readers learn from the So For Real series?

    The lesson is that it's okay to be unique and fearless! You can be a Christian and fab. Also, the people who appreciate you for doing YOU are the ones you want in your life!

Want more Nikki Carter?
Turn the page for a preview of
COOL LIKE THAT.
Available in March 2010
wherever books are sold.

"**M**om, come on! Mrs. Freeman is going to be here in a minute."

I seriously think that my mother is trying to make me miss my flight. Where am I going, you ask? To a summer enrichment program at Columbia University in New York City! How hot is that?

What's even hotter is that my bestie, Ricky Freeman, is going too. We get to stay on campus all summer long, taking classes and kicking it all over the Big Apple. Man, that's hot to the touch, okay!

My mom has been tripping since she found out that Ricky is going to the program instead of my other bestie, Kevin Witherspoon. Kevin got selected first, but his grandparents are really old-fashioned and they wouldn't let him go away for the entire summer. That's how Ricky got a chance to roll.

I know what you're thinking. Why would my mom have a problem with Ricky?

Well, the problem is not with Ricky per se. She's known him since he was a baby and we've been best friends since elementary school. We even go to the same church.

The issue is with the fact that it seems like overnight Ricky got super duper fine. He's tall, with caramel colored skin and big brown eyes, he keeps a low fade, his acne's disappeared, and he's got muscles he never had before. And check it. All that extra fineness is crushing on little ol' me.

My mom wants the truth, but she can't handle the truth.

She's been asking me questions ever since our debutante ball this past spring. Ricky was my escort, and I think that made her even more paranoid.

The killer part is, we aren't even dating. Not openly or secretly. Ricky suggested that we put our crushes on hold while we go to New York so that my mom could trust us.

In theory, it sounds like a good plan. Gia and Ricky— buddy-buddy, without a crush in sight. In reality it might be somewhat hard to execute, especially with all of the alone time we're gonna have.

Honestly, I think my mom didn't want to let me go, but she couldn't give me a good reason why I shouldn't be allowed to, after she'd already given me permission. She tries to be fair most of the time. Sometimes she comes up short, but mostly she's good.

The only thing that kicks rocks about this summer is the fact that my cousin and other bestie, Hope, won't be in New York either. I've promised to keep her updated by text, e-mail, and Facebook. With all of our technology, she shouldn't miss one second of all the action.

"Gia, do you have extra underwear?" my mom asks.

She's standing in the center of the living room, looking frazzled as I-don't-know-what. My mom is hereby prescribed a bottle of chill juice, for real.

"Mom, I've probably got enough underwear in my suitcase, that I won't have to do laundry once the entire summer."

"What about your cell phone? Do you have your charger?"

"Phone, check. Charger, check."

My mother sighs. "Okay, make sure you call me before your plane takes off. Then call me when you land. After that call me in the morning, once during the day, and before you go to bed."

She gets the are-you-kidding-me blank stare.

My younger sister, Candy, says, "Dang, Mama Gwen. When is she supposed to have any fun if she's doing all that calling?"

"This trip is not about fun, it's about getting her into a good school," my mother explains. "You've got money, right? And an ATM card?"

She knows that I have everything because we did a check, double-check, and triple-check yesterday. And the day before that.

She's tripping.

Finally, I hear Ricky's mom's horn blaring outside.

"They're here, Mom! I've got everything on the list, and if I forgot something you can FedEx it to me."

"Okay, Gia, give me a hug."

I give hugs to my mom, sister, and my stepdad, LeRon. They are quick hugs because we've already wasted enough time, and I don't want to be late for my flight.

My mom and LeRon follow me outside to the car. I knew they were going to do that, so I try not to get irritated, but I'm not sure if it's working.

"Hey, Gia!" Ricky says as he puts my suitcase in the trunk. "Are you kidding me? What do you have in here?"

"Clothes, shoes, hair products. The usual."

Ricky shakes his head. "It feels like you have ten sets of encyclopedias in there."

LeRon clears his throat. "Ricky and Gia. We've got some ground rules for you all while you're away for the summer."

Ground rules? I can already tell this is going to steal my joy.

"Number one, remember that you belong to God and that He can see everything you're doing all the way in New York."

Wow! He put the "God sees all" rule on us. If I was planning to hook up with Ricky or any other hot boy, that just totally killed it.

"Number two, have fun!" my mom says. "We trust you and know that you'll make us proud."

"That's all?" I ask.

Gwen cocks her head to one side. "I can come up with some more if you want."

My mom hugs me and Ricky one last time before we get into the car and finally pull off. Ricky's mother looks at us in the rearview mirror and smiles.

"I've got my own rule," she says. "Please go up there and act like you've got some home training."

This means for us to not do anything stupid that would end up embarrassing our families. That's a given.

I glance over at Ricky, sitting next to me in the back-seat. He's wearing the Tennessee Titans jersey that I gave him for Christmas last year. Cute. I'm wearing his gifts too: a charm bracelet and a butterfly barrette.

Yeah, Ricky went totally overboard last year with his gifting. He told me he was giving me the barrette because I reminded him of a butterfly. How is it that it seemed so much less corny the first time I heard it on Christmas Day?

I close my eyes and inhale deeply. Ricky's wearing some kind of cologne that smells really nice. Or maybe that's dryer sheets and laundry detergent. All I know is that he's smelling fresh and clean.

It's going to take all of my strength and the prayers of all the ladies in the church for me to resist the power of the crush. I really want to fight it, but without distractions from people at home, this could be the opportunity that Ricky and I need to finally make it official.

And of course, we've got to be official by senior year. Hello!

I feel the excitement building in my stomach as we pull up to the airport terminal. There is a flight attendant wait-ing on us at the door, since we're flying as unaccompa-nied minors. It almost feels like a babyish kind of thing, but when I found out that my mom wouldn't let me fly without the extra supervision, I gave up my issues with it.

With our escort (babysitter) we get to go through the security checkpoint without standing in line. Sweet!

Finally we're seated in the gate area until takeoff time, which is about thirty minutes from now. I'm about to plug in my iPod and listen to some Sasha Fierce when Ricky taps me on the shoulder.

"What's up, Ricky Ricardo?"

His eyes are wide and excited. "We're going to New York City. For the entire summer. No parents."

"I know, right!"

"Gia, this is going to be the best summer of our lives. We're about to make it hot."

I can't do anything but nod in agreement. Hotness indeed. Hotness to infinity!